1st Amer ed.   9 $\frac{95}{BC}$

D0483878

GIRL IN A TURBAN

GIRL IN A TURBAN

Marta Morazzoni

Translated from the Italian
by Patrick Creagh

ALFRED A. KNOPF   NEW YORK   1988

THIS IS A BORZOI BOOK
PUBLISHED BY ALFRED A. KNOPF, INC.

Library of Congress Cataloging-in-Publication Data

Morazzoni, Marta.
[Ragazza col turbante. English]
Girl in a turban / by Marta Morazzoni; translated from the
Italian by Patrick Creagh.
p.   cm.
Translation of: La ragazza col turbante.
ISBN 0-394-56115-5 : $15.95
I. Title.
PQ4873.0663R3413   1988   88-12688
853'.914—dc19

Manufactured in the United States of America

First American Edition

FOR TINA

Contents

THE WHITE DOOR

THEY LAID DOWN THEIR CARDS and stood up, leaving the empty, lustreless goblets on the table. The evening ended at the usual hour and the maestro, already on his feet, his eyes bright with wine, accompanied them to the door.

"We'll go on again tomorrow evening. You as well, Karl. We don't want to hear a word about your previous engagements."

They parted with a laugh of friendly agreement. The four of them came to visit him every evening, and for over an hour they would drink and play cards with the methodical regularity of those with nothing to do.

The maestro closed the door behind them, and in the silence of the large room still foreign to his habits he settled himself into the armchair. For some little while now he had found it hard to regain his breath after those long conversations with his friends; it was, in fact, an effort to get his words out, and to adjust his lurking hypochondria to the prevailing mood of good humour. He was frightened. He pondered with excessive anxiety on the delicate equilibrium of his body, which he felt to be malevolently threatened by some dark, hostile unrest. At times he found himself caught in a maelstrom of indefinable ailments.

It was growing dark outside, and no one had yet come to bring the candles. The large windows of the room looked out on to a garden obscured in its turn by an overcast day into which twilight was creeping step by step. He thought how infinitely he preferred the restrictions of his house in Vienna, facing on to other and identical houses. The vast space of this grand garden in which he was a guest was for all that no less acceptable to him, but he was upset by the random coincidence which in the very first days of his stay there had brought him mysterious signs of a tiresome malady. The extraordinary invitation had bewildered him in the first place: true, the hospitality had been lavish, but to the Villa he had not yet been admitted. For him they had opened up the apartments of a luxurious hunting-lodge at the far end of the garden. He had it all to himself, two storeys, low ceilings, large cool rooms and windows too big for the size of the house, so that it seemed to be all glass without supporting walls, open to the curiosity of all eyes; though in fact not a soul from the big house had ever passed by the lodge. Not even a servant.

They had told him that he would enjoy real peace and quiet there, and the invitation was intended above all as a magnanimous gift of tranquillity, to enable the composer at last to work in peace. His four friends only visited him in the late afternoon, when they thought he would have finished his daily quota of work. Even Constanze had not come with him, lest her restlessness, her fickle changes of mood, should disturb her husband's writing and prevent the effortless flow of music from the pen to the keyboard of the harpsichord. The brand-new instrument, of bewitching splendour, had been placed in a luminous corner of the drawing-room on the ground floor, between two windows giving out on to the dense foliage of the garden. The matt black and pearly lustre of the keys suggested an aristocratic privilege of quietude, such as the maestro had so long desired and requested. For years and years he had been forced to scrape by in hardship and insecurity, which he felt to be an unjust sentence, and at which in moments of courage he had managed an ironic smile, while in those of bitterness he had sometimes even wept.

His early youth had been difficult, troubled by the anguish of feeling himself trapped in a dimension without a future, and his natural vigour rebelled against this in fear and trepidation. While scarcely more than a lad, going every day to give lessons to Miss Rosa C., always treading the same route, he had for a while been convinced of a veiled warning about his destiny, a warning that came to him in a seemingly irrelevant form. One day he had seen the carcass of a dog on the grass by the road, crushed by the wheels of a carriage and pushed aside there at the roadside without anyone bothering to bury it. He had taken a good look at it as he passed, with a sense of compassionate solidarity. Its reddish coat was intact, without wounds, the pointed muzzle a little lighter in colour, the lips drawn back in a grimace, revealing white teeth. But the neck was unnaturally vertical to the spine: that was where the carriage had crushed it, and plainly it had not died at once.

He had looked at it the first day, on a sunlit afternoon. The next day it was still there, and the third, the fourth, the fifth. It stayed there a long time, exposed to the rains that drenched it in vain, and the sun that parched it with the same unproductive tenacity. The persistent beating of the elements on the unchanging carcass, always passive and motionless, seemed to him a sinister thing, and yet familiar. In days of black melancholy that dog was the static mirror-image of himself.

No one had come to bring the candles yet, and his eyes,

prying into the dense mass of trees outside the window, no longer discerned the least glimmer of light.

He tugged impatiently at the bellrope, for in the dark his malaise oppressed him unspeakably, and darkness and silence seemed hand-in-glove with his lurking dread.

At long last they entered with the lights. The two footmen who brought the candelabra were young, and noticeable only for the detached indifference of their movements, which made them seem ageless, even faceless. In the last remaining glimmer of light in the room they caught the dull grief in the maestro's eyes. Withdrawn and elusive, these seemed to divine, rather than to discern, the portents of an old age that in the course of nature should have been a long way off.

The two servants set the lights down on the large table and on the dark top of the harpsichord, then turned to the maestro with a brief bow before leaving the room. The maestro, for his part, watched the soft light gleaming on the wooden table-top. Since setting foot in the hunting-lodge he had not written a single note.

Morning came abruptly to the room, into which the heavy curtains let through not a chink of light. The new day entered, then, with the sudden sound of a carriage scrunching the gravel in the yard. The loud, hoarse voice of the coachman alternated with the high-pitched, imperious yapping of a petulant voice almost like a child's. A moment later Constanze crossed the threshold of the house and made for the still-dark room where her husband, half-buried in the armchair, had passed a troubled night, sometimes dozing and sometimes fretting about the weariness and ineptitude that he seemed unable to throw off. Before entering, with deft meticulous gestures she smoothed the rumpled material of her skirt, the dusty hem of which bore witness to the short stretches of road travelled on foot beside the carriage. Constanze loved these strange little walks, and preened herself on the extravagance of being escorted by an empty coach, as if she found in this a sign of her singular, if childish, capriciousness. On the other hand she soon wearied of such originality and, returning to the hard leather seat, she gazed around her, pleased with herself and happily worn out. Then, with swift, imperceptible movements, she kicked off her shoes and wiggled her toes beneath the spreading draperies of her skirt.

The maestro had only just recovered from the irritated astonishment caused by the din in the yard, when a flood of white light assaulted him with boisterous cheerfulness. In the unexpected dazzle he made out the figure of Constanze, smiling and radiant, the green travelling costume, and the broad-brimmed hat perched on her dark topknot of frizzy hair. The tubby, familiar form of his wife, unexpected and out of place in the gravely refined atmosphere of the room, brought him the alluring memory of the happiness they had shared.

To her cheerful, silent look he replied with a placated smile: so, she had come then, in spite of her inflexible determination not to be with him, for fear of interrupting his work. She had arrived alone, that at least, and with very little luggage – just the two cases and the large bag which the coachman had left at the door of the room. Rising with some effort from his chair, he went to her and kissed her lightly powdered cheeks, sincerely happy to have her with him. He was embarrassed for a moment by the woman's searching gaze: in the maestro's prematurely aged face, the dark bags under his eyes, she deduced sleepless hours and the fatigue of a labour which she too imagined to be unremitting and exhausting.

The scrutiny did not last long, as Constanze's frivolous, light-hearted chatter soon took its place, and she started on stories about the journey, gossip about their home in Vienna, and finally laughter and tears together as she told him about the two little ones, left behind in the Rauhensteingasse with their grandmother.

"There are no flowers in this garden," she remarked a little while later, taking swift sips at a cup of cocoa. She was seated by the window in the armchair which her husband had chivalrously yielded to her. He too, for the first time, noticed the many shades of green, all blending together in their uniform variety; but no other colour broke the light and dark of the trees and the grass, which ended only with the massive greyness of the big house in the background. But Constanze was the first to forget her own questions and remarks, as she turned from the garden to appreciate the sober, elegant interior of the room, the gentle light suffused from the windows upon the carpets and the graceful, gleaming furniture. Finally she went into ecstasies over the harpsichord, and wanted to hear its tone. At once! She made her demand with good-humoured brashness, but the maestro frowned, rubbing at his numb, stiff knuckles. He had never played on the instrument, and this was a poisonous secret which the walls of the room had so far kept to themselves. His latest work had come to a halt at the sketch of the *Dies Irae*, and he had dared go no further.

His voice sounded faint and embarrassed, even to himself: "Later, yes of course, but for the moment I don't think that . . . You know, I didn't sleep much last night . . . and you must be tired as well . . . You had such an early start."

"You didn't sleep?" She looked at him in perplexity. "You don't sleep, not even here? It's not like you – and with all this peace and quiet! Why, here you could hear a pin drop!"

"True enough, but somehow or other the nights have

[14]

become endless, and in between, when I do get some sleep, I have frightful dreams. Now that you're here I'd like to tell you about them, because . . ."

"Of course you'll tell me about them, but just at the moment it's your harpsichord I want to hear. Could I have a little go on it myself? No? All right, it doesn't matter, we'll play later. Maybe you'd like to take me outside. With a garden like this on your doorstep you really need someone to help you enjoy it."

The maestro listened to her, his head tilted a little to one side. He had always savoured voices, whether they rang out in high-pitched trills or sank into softer and more velvet tones. He was especially attracted to the variations and assonances of women's speech. He harkened to their conversations whenever he could catch an echo of them and, while disregarding the actual meaning of the words, would sense in them a kind of mysterious seductiveness. He would half-close his eyes serenely and slide into the infinite variety of the sounds, which for him were bodies susceptible to touch, voluptuous. Now he saw Constanze's damp lips tracing the line of the words, which betrayed her unawareness of his agonizing distress; but he willingly forgave her, content with the involuntary gift of that voice. Constanze was still talking as they went down the steps of the little porch, and she talked on over the soft crunch of the gravel beneath their feet.

They penetrated the lush green of the garden.

"You'll get a lot of work done here – it's a paradise." She sighed with an affectation of beatitude. "And what about the owners? Do you often go and visit them at the Villa? They're strange people, so they tell me. Just think – this is what the coachman said – they've had no one to stay ever since they've been here. You're their first guest, so you're the only one who knows anything about them. Isn't that true?"

She chattered on, stealing glances through the box bushes

to see if she could spy the austere outline of the big house, towards which she was attempting to move without making it obvious.

"I really am a guest without companionship," replied the maestro. "I have never set eyes on anyone from the house, and I've never been close enough to it to guess who lives there or what their style of life is. Your coachman is right, they're odd – and very reserved. Too much so. After all, I'd like to know whom I have to thank for these wonderful things."

Constanze was dumbfounded. She opened her wide, light eyes even wider than usual, eyes which were rendered a trifle expressionless by her rather sparse eyebrows. She laughed heartily, without taking her eyes off the stocky yet shrunken figure of her husband. She laughed enough to infect him with her gaiety. Then, struck with sudden remorse,

"You see," she said. "Maybe it's just as well I came to see you."

Their walk did not last long. The beauty of the garden, which had so appealed to Constanze's warm, good-humoured mood, appeared to lessen as they made their way further into it. The dense foliage formed an all but impenetrable screen against the warmth of the sun, the rays of which fell coldly through the thick green barrier, so that the young woman actually shuddered when she found herself beside a fountain gushing forth ice-cold water. Or at least it seemed less beautiful to Constanze who, unsettled and ill at ease, asked her husband to take her back to the lodge.

"You don't seem to be able to see the Villa at all from here," she said, put out and already a little petulant.

"You'd have to go a bit further to catch a glimpse of it. Anyway, it's not worth the trouble. I'm convinced that no one lives there."

"Do you really mean it?"

"Of course. I'm practically sure of it. You don't hear a sound, or ever see a living soul."

"Well, in that case we must go and look at it, at least from the outside, close to. We won't do any harm. And then, if you say no one will see us . . . It must be as beautiful as the archbishop's palace!"

In her animated voice the maestro recognized his wife's childish, suddenly enthusiastic curiosity. Her cheeks had taken on a slight flush, and her eyes were shining at the prospect of the breach of privacy about to be committed. He turned to her, tender and compliant.

"We'll try tomorrow," he said. "But there are still some railings before you can get near the Villa. You can't see them from here, but they're high, you understand, and won't be easy to get over."

"Oh well, we'll find a way. It won't be the first time you've tried to get in where you're not supposed to!" And she laughed a gay, sly laugh, her round eyes puckering up with delight; and without so much as consulting her husband she turned back towards the Villa.

"Constanze!" The imperious emphasis, the tone of breathless authority in the voice ringing out behind her, stopped her in her tracks. She stood stock still, without turning, her hands stiffening on the soft material of her skirt. Then, slowly, she turned her head, revealing all the astonishment and incredulity of a child's face, waiting for an inexplicable punishment. She looked him straight in the eye, and did not recognize his expression, as a rule so gentle. His eyes were glistening with a strange light, and the set jaw looked as hard as stone: impossible to believe that that command could have issued from the same lips that now, clamped tight, sealed in even the slightest breath.

Very slowly she retraced her steps, approached him warily, and waited in silence. The sudden mask melted from the maestro's face and his features resumed their habitual calm, sombre melancholy. His voice also was gentle again.

"I said, tomorrow. Now, when you've only just arrived, you must understand, it's not the thing. We'll have time even for that, if you really want it. And finally," he said, rather irked, "we don't have the right. They have treated me here with every consideration, left me in peace and not bothered me. I think I ought to behave with equal . . ." He realized that Constanze was not even hearing him. She did, indeed, continue to stare dumbly at him, but it was plain that her mind was trying in some way to work out a plausible reason for such sternness; and when she thought she had reached a conclusion, surprised by the truth she had finally arrived at, she frowned, and in a voice soured by the stridency of anger she drowned out her husband's words:

"How old you've got," she said, with all the savagery of a child who does not weigh its words. And she stalked off, martially erect, towards the lodge.

Thus Constanze had come upon the truth before the maestro himself. She had come upon it by the simple working (and she herself would have been unable to provide any deeper reason) of an instinct that saw beyond the rage of the moment and vexation at being forbidden something. She had lost a playmate; why she had lost him was not a thing worth wondering about. There was no turning back, therefore no point in going into the why and wherefore of the matter. The fact was irreparable, and all she could do was look out for herself.

With bowed head the maestro followed a few paces

behind, disconsolate and stricken by the unambiguous meaning of what Constanze had said. So, his malady was so obvious that it even had a name, and such a terrifying name at that: he was old, albeit not in years. How could this be? It was against all logic. Yet it was plain that the cheerful Constanze had, as it were, intuitively smelt a rat. He quickened his pace and felt his heart pound with the effort, but the woman seemed to have no intention of noticing his attempt to catch up with her. She had emerged from the thick of the trees and was marching, irate and indignant, across the sunny yard. She entered the house and went upstairs; a moment later her angry voice was heard ordering a servant to bring her luggage at once.

The maestro went into the downstairs drawing-room. The vague misgivings of the last few days had now become a certainty. He was ill, he was sure of it; and his sickness was eroding him inwardly, showing only imprecise symptoms for which he knew no remedies. He fell listlessly into the armchair, fumbling at his silk waistcoat with stiff, ineffectual fingers. He was short of breath and afraid of suffocating, while above his head Constanze's piqued footsteps went from cupboard to bed, from bed to cupboard, punctuated from time to time by the muffled thump of some object she had dropped in her fluster.

He thought of calling her, but the edge in her voice a while ago came back to him so sharply that any attempt to do so was stifled in his throat. Very soon the scuttling of footsteps also stopped, and the house sank back into silence.

It was already noon.

*

He longed for dark to fall. His eyes were wearied by the light, and he could no longer abide the violence of the sun in the room.

The younger of the footmen entered with catlike tread. He had not yet glanced towards the armchair, but it was enough for him, out of the corner of his eye, to catch the irritable movement of the maestro's hand, to send him hurrying over to seal the room in darkness.

Then he had a yearning for the light. His pupils dilated in the gloom, and partly from memory he reconstructed the shape of the room, fighting hard against the heavy, turbid sleep that was overwhelming him. He also visualized the still-immaculate white of the score propped against the harpsichord, and imagined it covered with the packed notes that were refusing to fall into place on the stave. The fact was that he could no longer think of anything except that heavy, swollen tide within him, that must either shatter into foam or choke him. Sitting as he was, leaning forward, he fooled himself into thinking that he could get rid of it. He was chalk-white and panting hard, his breath coming harshly in fits and starts.

He jumped with shame when he heard steps in the room, and turned his head towards the meek, flowing tones of Constanze's voice.

"I shouldn't have come to see you. It's obvious enough that you don't have much time for me." Her plaintive little voice then took on a rougher, sharper edge: "*However* glad I may be to know that you have a quiet time here, and are working well, and that no one disturbs you, not even your hosts."

She was silent for a moment, waiting, but as her husband appeared to have missed the stinging irony of her words, she continued more mildly.

"I'll give your love to the children, if you like, and say you're missing them. And that you'll be back soon."

"You can stay on, Constanze, at least until tomorrow. It's been a tiring journey for you, so why don't you rest a little longer? This evening, if you don't mind waiting a while, a few hours, perhaps I could play you something. At least a bit of the score that I've already got down."

But he spoke without conviction, listless and indifferent. Whether Constanze left or stayed on was of small importance to him, and the two alternatives were afloat in his mind like two foreign bodies in a whitish liquid. A sure instinct for life, on the other hand, forced Constanze away from him. She herself in daylight, and in health, saw him in the semi-darkness as a murky clot of ailments which she had to escape. But the more he repelled her the more she felt it her duty to conceal the fact under a pretence of fresh tenderness. Suddenly submissive, she bent over him, brushed his forehead with her lips and murmured something resembling a fake apology.

"Don't take it to heart, dear. I'm only leaving to make it easier for you to compose. They've paid you well for this job; don't let them down, and you'll see that things will take a turn for the better." The soft feminine tones pierced home, re-evoking in the maestro the indefinable joy of the affection he had felt for her.

"Au revoir, Constanze. When you next come, if you still want me to, I'll play you the *Requiem*. The whole thing."

His eyes had grown accustomed to the darkness, so that they distinguished the outline of the woman, and vaguely perceived her retreating by degrees, with deliberate slowness. She backed as far as the threshold, feigning a kind of sweet regret at this parting. In the dazzling rectangle of the opening doorway Constanze stood revealed. Just for an instant, then the dark grew dense again.

Half an hour passed, or more, after she left; and it passed in total silence.

"She's gone," repeated the maestro to himself, shaken by a fresh wave of apprehension, which underwent a change and emerged unexpectedly as melancholy. Constanze's rather tart, petulant voice had nevertheless been dear to him, and he was still touched by the tone of her farewell: insincere, of course, but as soft as silk.

His head was lolling sideways, aching, and his temples were throbbing hard, prompted by a slight fever that was in any case no stranger to his body. As a child, when he had toured half Europe like a circus animal to show off his prodigious talents, over-tiredness had sometimes brought on the same trouble. He remembered that the lethargy and fatigue which followed the pain were the first signs of well-being, and of the repose in which he would soon be cradled. Little by little the fear and weariness would subside, and he would watch them dissolve like a physical phenomenon quite distinct from him. It was the natural insouciance of a child that would bring him peace. He smiled inwardly as he remembered the joy of it, and contrasted it with the horror and emptiness that oppressed him now. He imagined it could not be later than three or four in the afternoon, and that the rest of the house was basking in the full light of day. He rang the bell on the low table by his side.

"Sir?" The voice of the footman answering the summons was respectfully interrogative and solicitous.

"What, have they got their ears to the keyhole?" thought the maestro. Then he regretted the meanness of the suspicion, and in a voice softened by an unspoken apology he asked: "Would you be so kind as to bring some light?"

Light was not a reasonable request in the middle of a sunny afternoon, but the footman, stepping back with an obsequious bow, started for the door without replying.

"Another thing . . .", the maestro checked him. "Would you have the gentlemen who will be here later informed that I fear I cannot keep them company this evening. I intend to work late."

The same mute assent, and the slender figure vanished with aquatic grace.

A little later, by the paltry light from the candelabra, the maestro was bent over the harpsichord, re-reading his score as if it were someone else's work, and discovering that this someone else was overawed by some kind of clammy terror. It seemed he had lost touch with the things and the people that had been close to him. Maybe this was what Constanze had been trying to tell him when, suddenly and spitefully, she had become his enemy.

He passed a hand across his eyes and endeavoured to think back to the time before the invitation to the Villa had bewitched him, trapped him in a blinding ray of light. On a sudden feverish impulse he thought that Constanze had been right: he had to get to the Villa and become acquainted at least with the house of his mysterious host. He would go tomorrow, and overcome the lethargy which his sickness had burdened him with.

Despite what he had said, he was not thinking of doing much work. However, when the footman went to the front door to meet the four friends, who had arrived at the usual hour, he let him send them away. He distinctly heard him repeat the formula which he himself had suggested, though in a toneless, monotonous voice. Then the footsteps faded out down the drive, and the front door closed in muffled quiet.

So the maestro did not work for long, and when the drowsiness that had been plaguing him all day finally got the better of him, he relaxed quietly in the armchair by the window. With one hand he raised a corner of the curtain, and contemplated the bleak and barely discernible colours of the late-evening shadows. The veins in his temples were pulsing violently, the strength in his hand ebbed away, and moment by moment the weight of the silk increased, until he could no longer hold it up. He was still conscious of the subdued noises of the household, and even had a feeling – perfectly absurd, of course – that he detected sounds from the Villa for the first time. When he slid into sleep he was in a state of childish excitement.

In sleep the sense of time eludes even the most alert of minds, to such an extent that one can float unawares into waking, and then into sleep again, without realizing when or how, or being conscious of the borderline. Sleep and waking meet in a region alien to the mind, a region where thought and reality join, where yearning and its consummation flow together at last. So it must have been for the maestro. He would never have been able to relate how the hours of that night unwound, or even to explain why at a certain point he had experienced such utter conviction that this was the moment, except that heightened feeling, in the air and in himself, had given him an unmistakable sign of it.

He had risen on tiptoe and, along with the faint squeak of his patent-leather shoes, heard the rustle of the satin of his long frock-coat. New suit and new shoes intimidated him, and the large, shining white door in front of him was far from inviting. There was no one to help him, and he was short and frail, despite the flushed plumpness of his boyish face, and the great embossed door-knob responded reluctantly to the effort of both hands together.

From the threshold of the darkened room someone had accompanied him, on a noiseless journey marked by very few words. From the gate he had seen the light green of a lawn sweeping up to the house. A series of broad, grassy terraces led to the foot of an ample breadth of steps, a stiffened fan of grey stone above which the Villa reared up in all its symmetry of tympana and columns.

From a distance, despite the majesty of the silence that enveloped it, the house seemed small and unnecessarily over-decorated; until, on reaching the first steps, where the grass flowed up and stopped at the touch of stone, he raised his eyes, and the dizzying solemnity of the façade filled him with awe.

A servant had come to meet him, raw-boned and hostile, wearing the black livery which the maestro knew well, and had motioned him up, with a glance of prohibition at whoever had accompanied him that far. The latter, without a word, had gently urged him on to the first step. After the soft moisture of the grass the maestro was afraid of that hard, cold touch, but he found that the sun had struck a measure of living warmth into the grey of the stones. He started to climb up slowly, without looking back, while the footman preceding him, rigid and withdrawn, showed him the way to advance without hunching the shoulders, with paces cadenced by some grave, slow rhythm.

He gazed ahead unseeing, divining the approach of the pillared portico at the top of the steps, while the light was gradually melting into growing zones of shadow.

When his mute companion stopped to wait for him he felt obliged to hasten his steps, becoming as breathlessly agitated as a child, so that his heart began to pound, and his cheeks flushed an embarrassed red. He was fearful of rumpling his suit, and spoiling the knot of the pony-tail in which his hair was neatly gathered at the nape of his neck. Shyly he tidied himself up and waited at the great dark oaken doors. They were only pushed to, and opened from the inside. A servant, identical to the one who had met him at the foot of the steps, now ushered him into a dark entrance hall, damp and oppressive. Gone was the solemn airiness of the columns, and the room appeared as a sombre, shapeless space, because his eyes, grown accustomed to the light, could not penetrate its depths, and searched for some glimmer that might lessen the cold that little by little was creeping into his bones.

It was plain that his flimsy satin suit, his silk stockings and lightweight shoes, could not protect him from the age-old damp that breathed upon him from the walls. He spotted a diminutive window, really no more than a slit in the deep stone recess. Through it filtered an oblique shaft of light that petered out before it could touch the floor. Instinctively he moved towards this strip of light, but the brusque rap of a stick on the floor made him draw back in fright. He had not noticed that this second footman was holding an ebony mace, strangely clumsy and without a knob on it. He would have preferred a word of reproof to that sharp rap of wood on stone; but the absence of voices seemed an inflexible law in there, and he choked back even the stifled cry that had risen instinctively to his lips. But he could not stem the tide of tears which glistened in eyes full of an animal sadness. In bringing him there, no one had hinted at this unjust severity.

He could not have said how long he had to wait in the gloom of the hall. He felt that the passing of the minutes, or of the hours, was breeding an unexpected patience in him; so that if the first minute had been long and terrible, and the first hour icy and atrocious, in time his body became accustomed to the cold, to the place, even to the silence. The numbness in his legs had spread throughout his body like a

[26]

pervading lethargy, while the desolating stream of tears had ceased. What remained was the wild melancholy in his eyes, but this had turned to a kind of fixed stare. Nor had the footman at his side given the least sign of life after that peremptory rap with his mace.

This, then, was the moment. While waiting he had unconsciously fixed his attention on the shining whiteness of the door which he had not so much as noticed when he came in. He had been staring at it for a while now, and by instinct he knew that there was the way and that was the ineluctable access.

He started towards it, certain that no prohibition would sound behind his back. He sensed the footman, stock still behind him, marking his steps and waiting, without offering help, while he opened the door himself.

The room he now faced was a large one, with a high ceiling full of light, the walls emitting a white lustre reflected in an endless series of mirrors. It was impossible to discern the source of so much brightness, which despite its intensity was mild and pleasing to his eyes, emerging from the torpor of the dark.

He entered very slowly, walking cowed and cautious over the white, bright edge of the flooring, which mimicked the reflections of the mirrors. Eyes fixed on the ground, he kept mechanically to the lines between the marble slabs of the floor, treading along them as if on a path grooved into a solid surface. The room had only two doors, one opposite the other, separated by an infinite space, or at least so it seemed. There was no furniture, and the curtains were honey-coloured and insubstantial, scarcely distinguishable from the whiteness of the walls and the glittering reflections of the mirrors.

He walked with caution. The lofty void of the ceiling sent

the creak of his shoes echoing round the room. He made his way towards the centre, while in addition to the faltering timidity of his first steps he felt apprehension at a new destination drawing ever nearer. He dared not glance at himself in the mirrors on either side of him: he was afraid of catching sight of his figure which, so scrupulously groomed and got up in new clothes, had certainly got dishevelled in the trepidation of the long, dark wait.

Passing his hands across his eyes, he hastily wiped away the last traces of tears. He was determined at all costs that no fibre of his body, however minute and frail, should lose its composure, or the dignified harmoniousness for which the whole had been so punctiliously prepared.

Just as the delay in the dark hall had been long and timeless, so now his passage across the room seemed to him immeasurably swift. Although he advanced with slow, short steps (he seemed in fact to be playing a game, pretending to balance dangerously on the dark lines between the marble slabs) the door was approaching rapidly. It was smaller than the one by which he had entered, and the handle was tiny and light to the touch. Seen from close to it was a simple door of hard, plain wood, with no decoration whatever; modest compared with the opulence of the room.

He heaved a deep sigh. The signs of premature ageing which had recently wrought a change in the maestro's child-like features were no longer to be seen. He reached the door handle without any trouble, and it was well that it cost him no effort, since all his energies were directed at controlling the convulsive palpitations of his heart and the labouring of his breath.

He opened the door and resolutely gazed ahead.

The boyish laugh that rose slowly in his throat spread forth in harmonious sound, while his body, shaken from within,

[28]

yielded with perfect ease to accompany the crystalline echo of his voice, which seemed to travel backwards across the room, through the dark hall, and down the steps beyond the colonnade, to shatter against the bars of the gate, at the end of the garden.

They say the maestro died at the first glimmer of the new day, which he may never have seen; indeed, the curtains were drawn tight shut. In any case, no one knows for certain the hour of his death, because that whole night long he was alone.

THE DIGNITY OF
SIGNOR DA PONTE

LORENZO DA PONTE had extremely lively, treacherous
eyes, a tongue both persuasive and predatory, and in spite of
wear and tear and the precarious straits in which he had lived
until he was nearly forty, he was a man to know what he
wanted; and by scheming away behind the honeyed guile of
a plausible face he succeeded against all odds in achieving his
ends; something he then never failed to brag about, when
occasion arose.

When he arrived in Vienna, aspiring to gain access to court,
he was neither famous nor established; he was no longer
even very attractive, for the regrettable accident which
deprived him of all his teeth had already occurred. His chin
stuck out and his lips were drawn in to hide the shame of his
toothless gums, so that his whole face seemed covered with a
fine tissue of minuscule wrinkles converging towards the cav-
ity of the mouth. His body, lanky and uncouth, was afflicted
with extraordinary thinness aggravated by the black clothes
which he affected, partly for the sake of originality and partly
due to his congenital shortage of money, which permitted
him only rare and thrifty changes of wardrobe. And yet his
proven experience of the world had somehow always helped

him, even in the worst situations. And it was helping him once again in that nest of vipers which was the dazzling Hapsburg court.

With brazen initiative, disregarding the formalities and the custom of the time, which required a proper spell of waiting at His Majesty's door, Da Ponte had moved slyly and side-long towards his goal. To attain this more easily he had fur-thermore determined not to scruple about toadying to the mediocre talents of Antonio Salieri, composer to the court. Indeed, he had become his faithful hanger-on and, in some bizarre way, even a friend. And lo and behold, he was now within reach of the radiant summit of happiness.

Salieri himself had sent for him, dispatching one of his ser-vants to the abbé's lodgings in the suburbs; and now, seated before him, Salieri came out with the request which Da Ponte had been ardently hankering after for months, yearn-ing for it in a fever of imagination.

"Your verses are not too bad at all, abbé. You have taste and fluency. Am I right in saying that your hand moves swiftly across the paper?" Salieri fell silent and glanced up, serious and requisitory, catching the glint of greed in the coal-black eyes of the other, who sat modestly poised on his chair; ready, however, to spring forward, like a cat crouching.

"Your Excellency is certainly more knowledgeable in the matter than I am, but this praise is not in keeping with the paltry value of the rhymes you have had a chance to see. Those are no more than the lowly efforts of a humble poet who would be glad to submit very different things for your appraisal."

He broke off, because Salieri's face was beginning to betray a certain measure of impatience. He was not, in truth, a man to dwell at length on praise of his fellow man, and now he had the feeling that Da Ponte's unctuous reply was an explicit invitation to confirm, in more forcible terms, what he had just said; while it had been almost as much as the aristocratic musician could do to voice that scanty display of praise, which he had no intention of repeating. Over the two of them crept a lukewarm silence, foreboding a perilous chill which the astute Lorenzo sensed in time. He reacted at once: settling himself more comfortably in his chair, he drummed his fingers very gently on the arm and spoke again, with more restraint and calm.

"In any case, we are not here to commend my handful of lines," he said. "Your Excellency's time is certainly too precious to be wasted on chatter."

This was a timely dyke thrown up against the rising ill-humour of Salieri, who seemed to regain a little colour (for a touch of rancorous pallor had set in around the lips), and who now returned to the reason which had caused him to send for this singular individual.

"I was telling you, my friend, that it seems to me your way of versifying might adapt well to music. If I am not mistaken, you should not have too much trouble in fitting a story to the notes."

This time Da Ponte made no reply, but feigned a profound absorption with which he filled slightly more than a minute's silence. Finally he looked at the composer with an implicit invitation to continue: the matter, he indicated, was of interest to him.

"This, in a word, is my project . . . and mind you, it is at the moment nothing more than a project, which I am not certain of carrying out. It was a hint from His Majesty that put the idea into my head, and I have been turning it over in my mind for some days. It is very true that I have not composed any operas for all too long, and, according to our Sovereign himself, I should restore some lustre to performances in the capital with a new production. These were the very words of His Majesty who, as you undoubtedly know, holds me in great esteem and is so gracious as to consider my music to be a creation worthy of his court."

Da Ponte conveyed his agreement by nodding profusely and smiling as broadly as his prematurely toothless mouth permitted. This was the inevitable ritual of self-congratulation in which Salieri indulged with reasonable frequency, before a select audience convened to share in that special and refined pleasure. The poet therefore postponed the liberty of showing the boredom which unfailingly overwhelmed him in such cases, and expressed his mechanical assent as best he could. Today's sacrifice would be well rewarded tomorrow, he thought to himself with far-seeing patience.

"Might His Majesty have suggested a theme for the new opera?"

"No, no, of course not; that is entirely my concern. His Majesty intends to trust wholly to my imagination and taste." Salieri's replies were becoming curt and suspicious. Perhaps he was changing his mind about this unusual Italian, behind whose apparent artlessness he now discerned considerable shrewdness, and whose insincere mask of submissiveness was beginning to get on his nerves. Except that . . . he had already got him there, had spent a precious half-hour informing him of that vague project of his, and could not just turn round and take it all back. All he could do was feel a trifle vexed at his own rashness, and not without some awkwardness go on with the conversation, which he felt less in control of than he would have liked. At least he was careful to restrain, as best he could, the brazen initiative of the other, who was, on the contrary, feeling reassured by the plain sailing of the conversation (ideas on the same subject are often poles apart!), and proceeded with giant strides towards the goal which he saw approaching more swiftly than he could have hoped.

"If I have not misunderstood," he said in a less submissive tone of voice, "Your Excellency desires me as a humble collaborator in this enterprise requested by our emperor."

Salieri inwardly assessed how far the good Da Ponte was from the least notion of humility, but for all this he found no way of retracting what he had so incautiously said. He nodded briefly, and before the other could start talking again with that maddening self-confidence of his, he managed to get out a curt excuse about an imminent, pressing commitment which did not allow him to prolong the pleasure of the conversation. He would himself make sure Da Ponte was informed when the project had taken on a more concrete form. Just now, he was extremely sorry but he must beg to take his leave. This unexpected interruption disconcerted our worthy poet. Despite this, he got promptly to his feet and began to sketch out in the air the preliminaries of a theatrical bow – which Salieri interrupted right in the middle by hurrying from the room.

"Eccentric and capricious, my composer friend," thought Da Ponte with a flash of pique, as he recomposed his features into their normal expression, now that the comedy of obsequiousness had been broken off with somewhat discourteous abruptness. But even so, the great step had been taken, and he was already court librettist. He felt himself to be such even before he had thought of a single word of the forthcoming opera; and in any case he had no reason to doubt the sequel to that promising colloquy.

When, a few minutes later, our poet left by the huge, dark-vaulted carriage-door to start on his walk home, there seemed to hover about him a most consummate pride; something, in fact, resembling a kind of ascetic ecstasy which

endowed this newly-elect to the divine privilege of fame
with detachment from the world and the narrow confines of
matter.

Persistent rain, intensified by lashing gusts of icy wind,
was falling on the cobblestones of the grey, deserted street.
The only pedestrian, he draped his cloak about him, hud-
dling into it as far as possible to keep out the cold, and drawing in his head between hunched shoulders to fight off the
keen bite of the wind. It was his custom to walk with eyes
cast down, stealing sidelong glances, and keeping one side
protected by the walls of the houses; for he considered that
mankind had too often taken advantage of his good faith for
him to abandon the habit of being on the lookout even before
the first sign of danger. Malicious tongues, on the other hand,
maintained that a bad conscience over certain past exploits
now made him go in fear of possible reprisals. The truth,
needless to say, lay between the two.

Our abbé, then, was walking with swift, springy steps
when, half hidden in the recess of an entrance a little further
on, he glimpsed a vague, dark form, not very tall, and so
muffled up in a wide brown cloak that one could not tell if it
was man or woman. It seemed to be waiting for someone, but
that was an odd place for an appointment, and the day was
inauspicious indeed for anyone obliged to wait in the open.
Da Ponte's proverbial caution tempted him to cross the
street, but the intent to avoid the encounter seemed too
obvious even to him, so he confined himself to moving away
from the wall so as not to collide with the waiting figure.

But he did collide with it, slightly, because the other
stepped forward with a clumsy movement and for an instant
pressed something flabby against his side. Da Ponte drew
back with a look of disgust and momentary terror. A barely
audible oath escaped his lips, addressed to this loathsome

[35]

thing, who said nothing, made no further movement, and did not even follow him with its eyes: for the hood pulled down over them rendered even the face amorphous. "Down-and-outs who don't know what on earth to do with themselves, and go around robbing decent people," thought our poet, quickening his pace, while his heart thudded madly against his ribs and the blood drained from his face, leaving him deathly pale.

Not very far ahead of him the street widened out into a square, in which there were generally carriages waiting outside the tall buildings that bordered it on all four sides. He was eager to reach it as soon as possible, even though he knew with perfect certainty that the hooded figure had not followed him. Had he had the nerve to look back, he would have seen it still there, motionless, shimmering with the raindrops which clung to the coarse wool of the cloak.

With some relief the fugitive entered the square. It was practically deserted, and the only two equipages to be seen were waiting at the main door of one of the buildings: the day was so grey and cold as to discourage even visiting and the taste for conversation. Steering a course down the middle, in spite of the lashing wind, he crossed the square and made for a street curving slightly to the left. He began to regain his spirits, the distasteful encounter with the beggar becoming more remote and vague, and almost forgotten when, half an hour later, he arrived within sight of his own home.

This was how he described a rather small and rather grubby room that he had taken in a suburban lodging-house owned by a capricious but kind-hearted woman who would occasionally pretend to forget that the rent was due, and who put up with certain delays that would have caused concern to a true hotelier. On the other hand, the place was a dump. The entrance was narrow and dark, and once the front door was shut it was hard to make out the bottom step of the wooden staircase leading to the upper floors, where the rooms had ceilings low enough to stifle you. But the lodgers had learnt the distance and the exact number of paces needed to reach that first step without stumbling over it, and had even taught themselves to manoeuvre adroitly in the constriction of their rooms.

Signor Da Ponte, then, made his way to his apartment, taking fresh heart at every step and inwardly feeling himself to be advancing with new dignity, which lent a tincture of reality to the idea of far more prosperous abodes. The last thought to cross his mind was what form to give his forthcoming work in verse; indeed, to be frank, he imagined himself as already moving in a time well beyond the one immediately awaiting him. In this future he envisaged another self, one pampered by fame and success, and so spoilt by these companions that his spirit was slightly sickened by them, tainted as it was by a slight hint of refined boredom.

But meanwhile, returning to the present, he needed to rest and revive. The cold had struck him to the very marrow, and maybe this was why his mind was wandering off in pointless fantasies, dreaming of the cushioned quiet of an elegant bed-chamber, or the discreet lighting of a fine drawing-room, which ended by resembling in all respects the elegance of the Salieri residence.

He opened the door of his room and a blast of damp, smelly air assailed him rudely. The window stood wide open, the fire was out, the bed was in wild disorder. A red tide of rage swelled up in his throat. He took a few steps back, leant over the balustrade of the stairwell, and shouted in a raging fury for the landlady. Every nerve in his body took part in that unbridled fury: stock still beside the door, he did not even think of going into the room and shutting the window.

[37]

He yelled again, with redoubled anger, since no one seemed to have heard him. Each passing instant of that silence provoked in him prodigious spasms of wrath, and the accumulation of this rage filled him at the same time with a kind of malicious pleasure.

Shuffling footsteps at the bottom of the stairs informed him that his victim had at last become aware of his presence.

"You know I don't want to hear this kind of hubbub in my house," came a cold, ratty voice without a trace of intimidation in it. "And you, my dear abbé, have very little excuse for raising your voice."

In the meanwhile she slowly climbed the stairs: so deliberately and insolently slowly as to madden a saint. She was a dumpy, slightly corpulent middle-aged woman, and her dulled eyes told of a tough, unresponsive indifference.

"I can no longer tolerate the neglect, the slovenliness, the insolence with which I am treated." Da Ponte now spoke in a very low voice, as if his rage had wound itself round his throat and paralysed it: the sounds came forced and strangled. "I pay you for this rat-hole that's not worth a penny, where the windows are falling to bits and blow open at the least puff of wind . . . Look!" He seized the woman by the arm and dragged her into the middle of the room. "Perhaps you can give this sort of treatment to the scum you put up for one night, but I'm not their kind, do you understand?"

The proprietress shook his grip from her arm: "Well, what d'you expect? So the window doesn't shut, eh? Then pay your rent and I'll send someone up to mend it."

Her client's anger collapsed, rag-limp. In a short while he wouldn't want for money, because the court cossetted its artists with ready cash; of this he was sure. But as things stood he had not a penny to his name.

Ah, what a dreadful thing is poverty, the unjust poverty of

a man of merit, now forced to stand in humiliated silence before a woman who had neither discretion nor delicacy! And one, moreover, who in this unfortunate situation was in the right.

Da Ponte came back to earth the instant he realized that the proprietress was claiming her due, and nothing more. The opera was not yet written, and indeed not even sketched out; and who could say if the man was going to compose it: who could say if Salieri, who had sent him packing so curtly and offensively, had ever had more than the vaguest intention of doing so? The shadow of a doubt crept slowly in, and the abbé inwardly experienced the disagreeable sensation of being nothing but a leaf in the wind, abandoned to the whim of a woman with no feeling. Without being aware of it, the poor fellow had dropped the arrogant expression which he had flaunted ever since the first words spoken in Salieri's drawing-room: words now so distant, and of so faint a sound!

"You haven't got a penny, I know." The woman looked at him steadily, straight in the eye. Then with a ring-encrusted hand she rummaged in her corset and drew out a purse of coarse but spotlessly clean cloth. She loosened the strings and took out some coins, which she put on the bedside table.

"I don't pay the carpenter for coming to mend the window. It's a matter of principle. You call someone, and pay him."

Her voice was rough and even impertinent, but Da Ponte, accustomed by necessity over the years to weighing and deciphering every least kink in the human character, thought that he could discern in it a kind of repressed gentleness. Certainly it was a tactful gesture to put the coins on the table, leaving them to his discretion, rather than forcing on him the mortification of holding out his hand; for in that case what little pride was left to him would have compelled him to refuse. The woman was not as coarse as all that, it seemed; and who knows, perhaps deep down she was attracted by the solitude and reserve of her client. This thought flashed for an instant into the mind of the poet, who hurriedly regained his composure, threw off his momentary embarrassment, and with gentlemanly dignity, and the slightest inclination of a head already flecked with grey, thanked his benefactress: "You will be repaid for your . . . generosity, in due time. That is to say, very soon."

The woman, who certainly cannot have believed the yarns of the most down-at-heel of all her lodgers, listened sceptically to this last piece of lunacy and, without comment, turned her back on him and went downstairs.

Rigid in the doorway of his room, the abbé listened to the heavy flapping of her slippers on the stairs until the final muffled thud. Then he closed the door, at last remembered the open window, pulled the two halves together and, jiggling this way and that with the skill of a carpenter, found a way to secure it reasonably well, stuffing a crack in the frame with a tight paper wad. Then he turned to the table, picked up the coins, counted them with ill-concealed relish and dropped them in his pocket.

Over the days that followed Lorenzo Da Ponte dissipated both time and capital in a lordly manner. Those coins that had fallen so unexpectedly into his pocket were, he reasoned, signs of the new, benevolent course of destiny, and it would have been churlish not to appear grateful for this, and completely trusting.

He would leave home in the late morning, shutting the door of his room carefully behind him, and go down the stairs announcing his presence by humming discreetly. If he happened to meet the proprietress he paid his respects with

sober gravity. His good luck stemmed from her, and he did
not forget it: but neither could he forget that she had been
nothing but an instrument of Fortune, the greater benefactress who now numbered him among her favourites. There
was therefore no need to go too far, to lavish compliments on
a landlady. Signor Da Ponte was a master of the art of keeping a proper distance between himself and those who did not
match up to the dignity of his rank.

So he left the house, as we were saying, and immersed
himself in the subtle pleasure of those long Viennese mornings, bustling with people labouring to brighten the waking
moments of the pampered nobility of the capital. He spent
much of his time in a small coffee-house, tasteful and moder-
ately priced, where he had occasionally encountered men of
some worth: or at least so they appeared to him from the
quality of their clothes and the insouciance with which they
partook of the matutinal delights of a Viennese pastrycook's.
Not that he had ever chanced to speak to any of them, or to
enter into their indolent and rarefied conversation. It was
enough for him to keep well in view, solitary, seated at one of
the more conspicuous of the small marble tables. In this way
he from time to time caught snatches of the conversations in
which he participated, as it were, in the abstract, with a sort of
total, even if wordless, affinity of spirit. That should have
been his world. But there was no longer any doubt that in a
short while it would at last become so.

On one occasion he even tipped a small coin to the waitress
when she put his steaming cup on the table. He did so
because the gesture seemed appropriate to the kind of place
and to his own standing. The girl, thanking him with a smile
that contained no trace of servility, took the coin as casually as
if it had been chocolate money in silver paper. But in fact this
munificent gentleman did not possess many more of such

trifles, and the savour of Viennese mornings grew daily more sour.

One could hardly say that Salieri was putting very much zeal and inspiration into drafting the new opera, even though it had been urged upon him by the emperor himself. That first conversation had had no sequel of any kind, despite the fact that days and weeks had passed. So time once more became of the essence to our friend the abbé, and the half-forgotten notion of doing some work became valuable too. His evenings, which he spent on the fringes of some approved aristocratic salon, had become insipid, tedious and lacking in any stimulating topics of conversation, while the road home seemed every evening a little longer and, even, more dangerous. The capital was becoming populated by haggard, dishonest faces that gave the wretched pedestrian little feeling of security.

But on one of those evenings, in one of those salons, he spotted a person who, he knew for sure, had connections of a business, if not of an artistic, nature with the court theatre; and this at last was a glimmer of light in the tiresome monotony of it all. He was a man of a certain age, careless in his dress, indifferent to formalities, let alone to cleanliness, but extraordinarily sure of himself. He behaved as if he owned the place, and could well have been the real owner just back from a long, dusty journey.

Now, however hard Da Ponte racked his brains for the man's name and connection with the theatre, he got absolutely nowhere. Our poet most certainly was not wanting in the kind of enterprise needed in such a predicament, and even he saw that to go directly to the person in question and find out who he was would have been a natural and obvious thing to do, especially in the worldly, easy-going atmosphere of a salon. But, owing to some ridiculous constraint, he dared not do so. He kept within easy range of his target, but without approaching too closely; in fact he practically avoided him when a face-to-face encounter seemed likely in the fluctuating dance of the conversation.

The evening wore on and midnight approached, the hour laid down for farewells, for compliments, for yawns stifled behind rustling fans and silken gloves. Da Ponte, more ill-at-ease than he could remember ever having been, and therefore all the more bitterly furious with himself, then hit on the solution – not so bold, but at least not entirely passive – of asking some other guest for information.

He approached a silent, uninterested-looking woman deep in an armchair which seemed engulfed by the black silks of her gown. Her indeterminate age and placidity of feature, heightened by the ample structure of her jaw, gave her a certain reassuring and maternal air. Da Ponte bowed and asked leave to sit beside her. The woman gave him an impassive look and gestured with her closed fan to an empty stool by her side. From close to, her age was more easily discerned, for although her matronly proportions made her look mature, and even past her best, the clear freshness of her complexion testified to the vestiges of a well-nurtured youth. She could not be much over thirty. But that placid imperturbability of hers was enough in itself to give the other pause: how was he to start a conversation? And even worse, how was he to steer it round to his point without making it obvious? For she now seemed the least appropriate person, so that his embarrassment was aggravated by vexation at his evident, irremediable error. Or this at least is how it seemed at first to the unfortunate poet.

"The peacefulness of these evenings, after all the bustle of the day, is a refreshing thing, don't you find, madam?" he began with scant enthusiasm, realizing at once that the adjective he had chosen sounded false to him, all the more so when the woman slowly turned her gaze and observed him with involuntary irony.

"Refreshing, would you say? Upon you, sir, one could scarcely say it has had that effect. You are extraordinarily red in the face, if you will permit me the familiarity." And she gave an easy laugh, without malice.

Da Ponte went along with her good humour, relieved on his part by the unexpected tone of cordiality. "The fact is," he said, "that the room is so crowded! I think this must be one of the most popular salons in Vienna. Every evening one comes across new faces." Aha! the trap was about to snap shut on his prey, and all so easy!

"There are never any new faces here," sighed the woman, languid and resigned. Her placidity was beginning to appear merely an Olympian façade behind which lay an enormous ennui.

At any other time her chance companion would not have failed to give her suitable comfort and to ease her sufferings, but at the moment he had other things in mind. He adopted, as far as possible, a frivolous, "salon" tone of voice.

"One has never seen that gentleman over there," he said. "The one now conversing with the countess."

"Good heavens!" exclaimed the lady in black, with genuine astonishment. "I think you must be the only person in Vienna who has never seen him. He is the manager of the court theatre, and better known in town than His Majesty himself!" And she laughed again, congratulating herself on the boldness of her wit. The naive remarks of her singular neighbour acted as a panacea for the tedium of the evening.

"So he frequents this salon from time to time." Da Ponte's tone was mid-way between a question and a statement, but the charitable lady was kind enough to confirm as much. Cer-

tainly he did, he came here often, especially since the countess he was now talking to was not, so to speak, a superficial
acquaintance of the theatre manager's, as he . . . The abbé
was not much interested in the gossip on this subject, at least
not at that moment; for on another occasion he would not be
the man to despise it. He vaguely followed the woman's
whisperings, and as soon as he discerned a pause he interrupted her chatter with discreet civility, steered her off the
subject and towards a stalemate in the conversation, and
then, with great charm and much ceremony, took his leave.

The woman, left on her own again, heaved a deep
sigh, opened her fan, and sank back into her former placid
indifference.

As for Da Ponte, he now found his mind in an unaccustomed turmoil. He pondered and weighed the expediency of
introducing himself to the man as the librettist of Salieri's
new opera. In this way he would achieve the double aim of
finally discovering how much foundation that vague project
really had, and of linking his name permanently with it. It
was an extremely bold act, he realized, but at the same time a
conclusive one; and at this he cast aside all doubts and went
into action, without even giving himself time to work out a
plan in more detail, so as not to snuff out what little courage
he had summoned up.

He directed his attention towards a group of men in
animated conversation and, pretending to have noticed
among them some special acquaintance of his, set out to join
them; but in order to reach them he had to pass right by the
manager and his beautiful companion. One step from the
couple he made a diligent, deep bow to the woman, with a
show of surprise and pleasure at finding her in his path. He
was met with a cold nod which implicitly discouraged all conversation. Da Ponte, however, had his own way of attracting

[45]

the attention of those who did not yet know him, a certain mysterious air of magnetic complicity that enveloped his prey and unfailingly lured them into the net of curiosity. The manager proved no exception, and did not escape the trap: the thin, black figure of the abbé attracted him by the mixture of impudence and humility which one divined from his features and behaviour.

"My dear, would you be so kind as to introduce me to your guest?" The countess did so grudgingly, for she had no great liking for a man whose insistence as a petitioner she already knew. Cursorily and sarcastically, stressing his gift as a great talker (a valuable gift in a salon, especially at that time), she introduced Signor Lorenzo Da Ponte, from Italy.

"From Ceneda, sir," the abbé emphasized. "Italian, like Maestro Salieri, whose unworthy poet and librettist I am. But perhaps Your Excellency is already *au courant* . . ."

His Excellency turned out to be anything but *au courant* in the matter, and in fact showed some surprise. "But then," he added, "ever since our emperor discovered his vocation as a patron of the arts he has bothered less and less to tell us about new talents arriving in the capital. And you, I take it, are one of these. But tell me, what are you preparing for our theatre?"

This question caught the librettist on the wrong foot, and he mumbled something about an event so outstanding that he could give no advance information without the risk of detracting from its impact.

"Come come, my dear sir, one doesn't make mysteries of that kind with me."

"Not with you, of course, but the countess . . ." and Da Ponte smiled courteously and affably at the visibly piqued noblewoman, "has the right to enjoy the surprise in full!"

The manager bowed in acknowledgement of the poet's quick thinking, while the latter heaved an inward sigh of

relief, excused himself for having to leave the question unan-
swered, made his farewells and melted away among the
guests, gaining the lobby and thence the main staircase without any further pauses.

On the way home he pondered bitterly on the stupid
fantasies he had indulged in all those months, waiting for a
summons that would never have come. He had senselessly
wasted time, and in addition had lost his opportunity, perhaps for ever, whereas he ought already to have made a move
and prepared the ground, however hard and arduous.

The next day, at last, he acted.

He left the house quite early that morning, and forbore to
dally at the usual coffee-house. Instead, he made for the elegant, secluded quarter where Salieri lived. Having crossed
the spacious square, he turned down the cobbled street that
ran out of it. For an instant he again felt that triumph which
he had savoured with such thoughtless anticipation; but
simultaneously came the repulsion of his collision with the
beggar, and it was as if he saw him there again, and felt the
same nausea and terror. The street was peaceful, and the
houses on either side might have been empty, so quiet were
their inhabitants. Despite its class and exclusiveness, the
place was far from pleasing to our troubled poet.

He turned in at the main entrance of Salieri's building,
went up to the first floor and knocked at the door of the apartment. He waited for quite a while before the butler, a very
haughty and overweening individual, came to open the door.
Da Ponte's request to be received by the famous musician
must have had to travel a great distance before reaching its
destination, seeing that the visitor was left standing in the hall
for a good half-hour, but at length he was ushered into the
drawing-room, and for the next half-hour he could wait in
more comfort, seated on a hard chair.

Salieri entered, cold and quite openly irritated by the visit and, without apologizing for the long wait to which he had subjected the abbé, took a chair facing him.

"I am sure Your Excellency can imagine why I am here." The uncertainty of the poet's voice betrayed unease and a vague sense of dejection. "I should like to make it absolutely clear that I am at your disposal in the matter of this opera, following our agreement of some time ago."

"Agreement?" The composer was somewhat taken aback. "I had no idea that we already had, as you put it, an agreement. Be that as it may, you must understand that I am at this very moment getting ready to leave for Paris, and was no longer thinking of carrying out that project, least of all in such a hurry."

In a different place, speaking to a different man, Da Ponte would willingly have allowed himself to fly into a rage, that mad, remedial rage which he flaunted from time to time like a piece of theatrical bravura. But here he held himself in. His reply, indeed, was calm and restrained. He said that the time which, due to a series of fortunate coincidences, he now had available, would only be so plenteous for a short while to come. If, therefore, His Excellency wished to avail himself of this lucky circumstance, and if the opera they had spoken of was still among his desiderata, then in a word, perhaps . . . it would be unwise to let the opportunity slip.

Salieri made no reply and Da Ponte, for his part, dared insist no further. The silence grew ponderous and stubborn on either side. It fell to the less tenacious of them to give way, and Salieri, with little conviction, said, "Then it's up to you to think of a subject, abbé. When I get back I will set it to music, if I find it suitable."

"If you would care to make some suggestion about it . . ." His hold was precarious, and he had to cling to it with the strength of desperation. But little came of this: the composer had already conceded too much, and too reluctantly.

"See to all that yourself, my friend, as it seems to be so important to you. I reserve judgement until the work is finished."

Da Ponte gave him a look of unadulterated loathing, but there was nothing for it but to thank him deferentially and back towards the door. It was clear that Salieri no longer had any serious intentions in the matter, and that only the persistence of the librettist (at last the poet's tenacity had truly earned him that title) had extracted the commitment from him, but at the price of undying mutual contempt.

Indeed, if Salieri came out of it exasperated by the abbé's intrusiveness, the latter took the road home inwardly cultivating an evil, venomous rancour, and the memory of each and every word of that ill-starred conversation only added fuel to the flames.

He had taken no more than a few steps along the deserted street when he once again saw the bundled-up figure of the beggar, this time a little closer to the door of Salieri's building, so he hurriedly crossed the road (he had no compunction about showing that he wanted to avoid the encounter), thinking that the man must be intensely stupid to stand begging in a street where no one ever passed: "Unless, poor fool, you live on the charity of Signor Salieri, in which case you deserve to starve in this world and the next." The rage smouldering within him was such that, without realizing it, he muttered this nasty remark out loud, mouthing convulsively as if uttering a prayer to the devil.

All day long he wandered aimlessly around the streets. The idea of his rat-hole of a home distressed him, but he was also troubled by the thought of making conversation in a salon, and of mixing with people who would read the mortification and disappointment written all over his face.

He dawdled for a long time in the street leading to the countess's house, but he did not cross the threshold. He passed it and made his way to the imperial palace, roaming around that neighbourhood looking lost and unhappy. He hung about like this, doing nothing, until the streets were practically empty of people and carriages; then he made for the outskirts.

He was deathly tired, weighed down by profound, forlorn disheartenment, and to rub salt in the wound came the jeering memory of a more friendly and congenial Vienna, the one he had looked fondly upon before experiencing its deceits at first hand. In his mind he compared the unfriendly picture of the capital with the dignified, good-natured familiarity of his homeland in the Veneto. But only for a moment: Da Ponte had nothing if not a sense of reality.

He sat up all night long, throwing himself on the bed only when the sky was already growing light above the rooftops. Then a leaden torpor got the better of him, and at last he fell asleep. He slept all that day and through the following night, waking from time to time only to sink into drowsiness and then once more into sleep.

Two days later he set to work. He worked unceasingly for three weeks, leaving the house only in search of something to eat, which he brought back to his room; though from time to time, usually in mid-morning, he descended from his disagreeable retreat, which he detested all the more now that he was constrained to live in it, and walked up and down in front of the coffee-house in which he had been so welcome only a short while before. However, he did not go in, for now he was short of cash and, more important, no longer possessed the patient docility with which, in that place, he had carried through the long wait for fame and riches.

The Dignity of Signor Da Ponte

Of the work he did during those weeks we can only say that he detested it as one detests a treacherous enemy and a gaol-mate. The words which formed up in ranks on the paper gave him no hopeful glimmer of the success he had come to idolize. It would not be this rubbishy plot that would earn it for him, a plot that couldn't stand on its own feet and would have to be propped up by the efforts of a heedless and hostile composer. Yet Da Ponte worked, weaving and stitching up the story, careful at every turn to pander to the frivolous tastes of the court audience. For even now, shut up in his room, there was no escaping from dependence on a world that held him in a tyrannical grip.

He waited patiently for Salieri to return from Paris. He waited in his ante-chamber to be received by him. He waited for two months before hearing a word about the manuscript.

Contrary to all expectations, the word was positive. One of His Excellency's lackeys paid another visit to Da Ponte's lodgings, bearing a crisp note from the composer summoning the poet with all possible urgency to the court theatre: in less than a fortnight the opera must be ready, and they must speedily sort out the remaining incongruities between the libretto and the musical score.

Da Ponte flew to the theatre, where Salieri, waiting impatiently for him, without so much as looking him in the face pointed to the score, on which the ink was still wet, and indicated the places to be corrected or honed down. He must get to work at once, there in the wings, change the ending, make it less wordy, cut out all that verbose, useless phraseology. At first, Da Ponte felt he could not even grasp the composer's icy, hurried words; but finally he understood, agreed to everything and, taking a pen in a hand trembling with excitement, carried out the maestro's instructions to the letter. By his side the court music-copyist worked equally feverishly to fill fresh sheets with the parts corrected by the poet, who did not know and did not dare ask himself the reason for all this rush; just as he did not care to enquire into Salieri's irritable stand-offishness.

He worked all that day, and at the end of it was told to come back next day; which he did most punctually, not neglecting to inform his landlady, on whom, however, the word "theatre" made no impact whatever. As he stepped out briskly towards his destination the poet consoled himself by thinking that he would not have to put up with such crass ignorance for much longer.

Salieri had new and even more pressing criticisms to make of the libretto, and in less than ten days Da Ponte to all intents and purposes had to rewrite his work from scratch, passage by passage; but he was far from being upset by this. As the work went on he felt inwardly more and more encouraged, and Salieri's nervous hysteria, rather than being intimidating, ended by amusing and stimulating him. At last he caught that wondrous savour of fame, desired for so long and pursued with such labours; and it bewildered and intoxicated him.

As things turned out, the opera, performed in the court theatre on a gloomy October evening in 1784, was a sensational fiasco.

For the third time Lorenzo Da Ponte went to pay a call on Antonio Salieri. Little more than twelve hours had elapsed since the bitterness of that ill-omened debut, a night during which neither of the two protagonists had found any relief in sound sleep. This time, oddly enough, the poet had to serve no time in the ante-chamber: he was admitted at once to the drawing-room, where he found the composer standing before the fireplace. He had his back to the door, and in his hands, clasped behind him, he held the manuscript of the opera. Da Ponte stopped in the doorway, waiting. He was waiting for the storm to break, but had no idea what form it would take.

Slowly Salieri turned. He looked him in the eye without a word of greeting or a gesture of welcome. The vicious hostility evident in his face betrayed a malevolent relish for inflicting pain, which at that moment governed him even more than the snub and humiliation of the previous evening.

"Signor Da Ponte," he said at last, "will be so good as to recognize that he contributed to this glorious outcome with extraordinary zeal. I believe I had to struggle against monsters of slovenliness in order to set these lines of his to music."

The other could find no words to rebut this infamous accusation, though he would have liked to object that those poor verses had in fact received the composer's summary approval. In vain did he make a feeble, clumsy attempt at shuffling off the chief responsibility for the failure on the restless unruliness of the audience. If the gentlemen in the audience had paid more attention to the plot, if they had listened . . .

"They listened all too well," snapped Salieri, "and they will not forget in a hurry. As for me, I fear that in future I shall not be able to have the pleasure of your assistance." He looked hard at the abbé, drank in the full measure of his humiliation, and added with enormous mockery, "But Vienna will not be without other musicians who aspire to link their names to yours. And one more thing before you go: the theatre manager, who told me he met you on some occasion or other, is expecting you to call in for your wages for those few days of work. That is all. Goodbye sir, and good luck." The nod with which he indicated the door allowed of no dissent.

Da Ponte was annihilated, more so now than he had been the previous evening in the theatre: annihilated and shaken by impotent, smouldering wrath. He felt it boiling riotously within him, seeking an outlet in the bitter, shameful tears that stung his eyes. He hurried down the marble staircase and rushed into the street, as if setting out in his turn to find a victim to take revenge on. And indeed he found one, bundled up in the threadbare brown cloak that entirely concealed his form.

Da Ponte flew at him with the speed of lightning, grabbed him at the base of the neck and began to thrash at him with inhuman force. He drove his fist into the chest and face of his luckless victim, who managed only a few feeble, ineffectual attempts at defending himself. The aggressor's ferocity seemed to increase all the more as he felt the beggar giving way helplessly to his violence. The wild blows thudded dully on the man's body and his face was already a mask of blood, but the other went on striking, one hand supporting the dead weight which would otherwise have slipped to the ground. At last the victim collapsed, with a long, low moan like the inarticulate whimpering of the dumb, answered by the deep, hoarse panting of the aggressor, who only at this point stopped striking and stood, legs wide apart, propping himself with one hand on the wall. So he remained for some time, exhausted, gazing at the heaving, blood-soaked bundle at his feet. Then he walked quickly away, without looking back.

This episode was only a very brief interlude in a series of vivid incidents – the poverty of his early times in Austria and the success which later, and at last, smiled upon our poet. Indeed, it is no coincidence that, in the long, detailed autobi-

ography of Abbé Lorenzo Da Ponte of Ceneda, this disagreeable setback and its regrettable aftermath receive no more
than a summary mention of the none too successful outcome
of the first performance of *Il ricco di un giorno*, music by
Antonio Salieri.

After all, the long life of the Veneto poet was destined to
include so many triumphs, and so many other bitter
adversities, that this marginal glimpse of Vienna life was
bound to sink into the mists of a memory increasingly faded
and unstable.

It is true that, for quite a while after the episode, Da Ponte
occasionally remembered it with an acute sense of malaise; a
malaise which throughout his adventurous life revisited him
from time to time; but in isolation, without any relation to the
particular occasion that gave rise to it. In the end it was no
more than a wasp-sting that sometimes still took him by surprise, and for an instant altered the character of his face. But
only a very close observer would have spotted the signs.

It may be that, if in some way the abbé had learnt that his
unknown victim's wounds had slowly and with difficulty
healed, the sudden, involuntary shudder might have vanished altogether. But news to this effect never reached him:
nor, for his part, did he make the least move in the matter.

GIRL IN A TURBAN

TOWARDS THE LAST YEARS of the seventeenth century, in the little town of Scheveningen on the doorstep of the magnificent Hague, there lived a merchant. He was at that time a man nearing forty, fine-looking and with distinguished, generous features, evidence of solid and abundant wealth. Though without hauteur, his tall frame and dignified bearing might have been intimidating at first, but it swiftly revealed a captivating gentleness of manner beneath all that sternness, especially when he let himself go in conversation, an art in which he excelled by nature. In fact he took rare pleasure in talking, and possessed the gift of never wearying the listener. Now that he was traversing the fullness of maturity, and a life already so rich in events and memories prepared him for a future even more vivid and prolific, this gift (for which he had been remarkable from his youth up) was attaining its zenith.

It was only a few years since he had made up his mind to embark on the marriage which his father, on his deathbed, had warmly urged on him, so that he should not ossify into an old age without heirs to whom to pass on the treasures of his good nature and the flourishing business which he in his turn had inherited. For some time, despite the warm tears with which he had sworn obedience to his father's last wishes, he had shunned feminine company, preferring to live alone in his parents' large house, dark and encumbered as it was with massive pieces of furniture which he had not wanted to touch, either from laziness or owing to affection for and loyalty towards the past which they with discreet tenacity embodied. He had moved nothing but the large oaken table, which had been shifted from the middle of the room to a place near the west window. There our merchant would sit in the late afternoon, when work on the accounts, the registration of goods, and the debits and credits of the day kept him busy for long hours. The waning of the day was the time set aside for this task, and therefore he stole the last glimmer of light from the sunset, reflected off the sea in reddish or faintly bluish streaks. In front of him, a few hundred paces away, were the pale yellow beach and pearl-coloured water which Jan (for this was the merchant's name) had known since boyhood.

There, in that house, years and years earlier, his father had chosen to live, gladly exchanging the comforts of the city for the convenience of being able to follow the comings and goings of the ships at first hand, and to oversee the dispatch of his merchandise, which frequently he had not hesitated to accompany on the longest and most perilous voyages. His crates, in fact, contained unusually rare and precious materials; for Master Bernhard Van Rijk, picture dealer, did business with the finest artists in the Netherlands, and his contacts extended as far as the nobility of the distant courts of northern Europe.

Indeed, when Jan was about to be born, in 1658, his father had embarked on one of those voyages.

If he had to travel a long distance by sea with a cargo of

pictures, the prudent Bernhard habitually planned his itinerary down to the last detail. He provided with parsimony but without stinginess for the needs of the voyage, and above all was careful to leave nothing outstanding, either in his household or in transactions which he still had in hand. He loved and cared for the wealth and welfare of the family as a precious gift which should not foolishly be put at risk. This is why the days preceding his departure were such a bustle.

With precise, straightforward orders the master left each one of his employees with the tasks which "in case of my death – God's will be done! – you will succeed in carrying out to the benefit of yourself and of my house".

In that same room where, years later, Jan drew up the daily balance-sheet, the old Van Rijk (though not old at that time) directed and controlled the intricate tangle of transactions to which he owed his affluence; and before that table, on the day before his departure, his servants and two assistants presented themselves in turn. Last of all came his wife, and then the door closed behind her, leaving the couple together in peace, to agree on what remained with regard to the household arrangements which she, in her husband's absence, had to take over entirely. It was hard for Master Bernhard to saddle Miryam with all that responsibility, but he had assayed her prudence and her vigour over years of marriage, and he trusted her in everything: he knew her to be staunch both in joy and in misfortune. The role that fell to her was not an easy one, but it was the destiny common to so many women of her station: to make sure that the days went by in an orderly manner, to regulate the rhythm of the weeks, if not of the months, aware of the benefits brought by those voyages and separations, but also of the risks which they entailed.

It was, then, on a June evening in 1658 that Miryam stood in the doorway of the room, waiting. The two young assistants were still in the room, and they greeted her deferentially though without missing a single syllable of what their employer was saying to them. They were dismissed almost at once, and Master Bernhard beckoned to his wife to enter.

When she had closed the door the room seemed darker, in spite of the light from the candles and the last gleam of sunset filtering through the panes of the great window, so that in the half-darkness the golden yellow of her dress glowed with a deep intensity. She walked slowly and carefully, with a trace of awkwardness, although she was only in the fifth month of pregnancy; but it was her first, and the strange uneasiness which this unaccustomed condition wrought in her compelled her to move with extreme caution.

"You have acquired the gait of a princess," said Bernhard with gratification, for even in the smallest things he recognized his wife's prudent wisdom.

But the eve of departure of which we are speaking was an unusual one. If in outward show this departure seemed the same as so many others, as the two of them bent over the papers which they were studying with intense concentration, their spirits alternated between the contrasting emotions of reciprocal tenderness and a certain tacit resentment. Coming to the threshold of her first confinement when no longer very young, the good Miryam found it hard to suppress the notion that her husband, in abandoning her at a moment of such uncertainty, had no idea of her fears and anxieties. Like most women in her situation, first child or not, she was afraid, and indeed peevishly convinced, that she would die of it; while to Master Bernhard the matter seemed to be entirely in the course of nature, and to require nothing but a patient waiting upon the event. To this we should add that the daily pressure of business distracted him from other, and more weighty, reflections. Recently, indeed, he had observed in his wife only her splendidly flourishing appearance, enhanced just now by the delicate perfection of her dress and the simplicity of the hairstyle framing a face which was, to be sure, somewhat pale, but not over-fatigued. Pregnancy had still further ennobled her features.

"Well then, have you any other orders for while you are away?" asked Miryam finally, after listening for over an hour to her husband's directives.

"Orders, no. But I would recommend you to avoid excessive exertion and worry. I shall be back in time to see our son come into the world, and there's no reason for you to fret so much now, for I clearly see you are not easy in your mind. You know that my voyage will be over in less than two months. Besides, my presence here will only be a hindrance when the moment comes."

But this last thought he kept to himself, for with patronizing forbearance he considered that the woman was not capable of understanding, let alone sharing, the subtle pleasure which the thought of the journey roused in him at that moment, and in those circumstances.

In point of fact Master Bernhard was always glad to get away. Not that he was not fond of a quiet, orderly family routine, of which indeed he was the stern and inflexible guardian, and even now he did not fail to look forward to that birth with legitimate pride. But his love of his job, the fervour with which he accompanied the works of art that had been entrusted to him and, last but not least, the relish he took in profit, in the money which it seemed to him he acquired in more noble a manner than did so many others who, like him, were involved in commerce: all these things together appealed to his reasonable vanity and urged him towards mild adventure, which even in these circumstances he did not care to relinquish.

And then, the expedition he was setting out on was an unusual one. He would take nothing with him but one small canvas, the value of which, Master Van Rijk was convinced, was extraordinary, and destined to increase in the near future. As for the uncertainty of the transaction, which he was by no means sure of being able to conclude, this did not seem to him sufficient reason for shirking the discomforts of the voyage. At the most, well, perhaps he might take a few other things of lesser value, easily marketable and immediately remunerative. For the sake of that small, inestimable gem, which as time passed he had come to love as he might a living companion, he would have risked far more.

Contrary to his usual practice he had kept the painting at home, rather than in the warehouse. Propped against the wall opposite the window in the bedroom, the picture by this time had reigned supreme for a month, and had become familiar even to the maids, who had strict orders not to lay a finger on it or shift it an inch from where it was. No one outside the Van Rijk household had ever seen the picture, for it had been offered to no one. The destiny of the painting, at present confined to the silence of a single room, was replete with mysterious promise, with a radiant, exceptional future. Only Master Bernhard, as he looked at it every evening before retiring to the double bed in which he slept alone (Miryam's condition made it advisable for her to withdraw to a more secluded room, in the company of a maid ready to act upon the least sign from her mistress), bestowed on it a jealous, paternal tenderness. All in all, therefore, it was by no means unnatural that Mistress Van Rijk occasionally caught herself contemplating the presence of that painting in the house with a certain unspoken rancour.

We were saying that the voyage which the good merchant was about to make was not a little risky: impossible to predict the outcome, for the precious picture might well return to Holland together with its guardian, without a penny earned to recompense the exertions and upheaval now in preparation. In this respect Van Rijk was exceptional, both as man and as merchant; for where no one else would have embarked on adventures that were not guaranteed to bring in a good fistful of florins, he cheerfully and enthusiastically faced the risk, inwardly cherishing the secret pleasure of the unpredictability of events.

The target of the endeavour was a Danish nobleman with whom Master Bernhard had for years kept up a regular correspondence and to whom, to their mutual benefit, he had already dispatched a number of very valuable works of art. The two of them, however, had never met, so that now, on the basis of that painting, the Dutchman thought that the moment had come to put to sea (a voyage in any case neither too long nor too dangerous) and to present himself in person, as the guardian and guarantor of the work which, with deep instinctive conviction, he loved to the point of finding it hard to part with. Indeed, it was only the respect in which he held the lord of Herfølge that had persuaded him that there the work would be in the right hands, and far enough away for him to feel no worse than an impossible nostalgia, once the parting had taken place.

A month before making ready for the expedition he had written a long letter to his correspondent informing him of the reasons for his journey, describing the virtues of the masterpiece that he had kept for some time in his own hands, and offering to demonstrate its worth to him, if only for the pleasure of sharing with an art-lover the splendour of a painting which, in both workmanship and inspiration, was in his opinion without a peer.

The reply arrived in due course, three weeks later:

Dear Sir,

The eloquence of the passion with which your letter describes this miracle of painting does not allow of my delaying any longer in inviting you to my house. You will be welcomed here as an old friend, and I make no secret of the fact that the pleasure and suspense with which I await you not only concern the work which you have promised me, but extend also to yourself, whom I shall at last have the joy of meeting. At whatever time you arrive, you are to feel expected. I imagine that the vessel will dock in the harbour of Holbaek, and from there you will have no difficulty in reaching my estates. The season in which you will arrive, if the date of your departure remains unchanged, should be thoroughly favourable: the weather is already fine and clear, and is becoming gradually milder after the winter storms. You will be my guest for as many days as you wish, as far as is permitted by the condition of your lady wife.

Your devoted friend,
D. v. Herfølge

When this reply reached him from far-off Denmark, Master Bernhard laughed with secret satisfaction. He at once looked for a ship to take him there, prepared his baggage, and last of all packed up the canvas with tender care, refusing help or advice from anyone in this complex and delicate operation.

Miryam herself was forced to observe, while speaking to a maid one day, that her husband seemed younger, years younger, and as excited as a boy before his first adventure.

"Men are like that, madam. They go off without a thought of what they leave behind. Ah yes, they are too sure of finding it there when they come back." And the maid shook her head disapprovingly. But Miryam had no ears for such things. She herself felt calmer, close to a kind of liberation: the painting was finally leaving the bedroom and would never return there. Of this she was certain.

The day of departure arrived. When Master Bernhard awoke early that morning, in spite of the fact that they were in the heart of a mild, promising June, the sky was still dark and the sea dulled and indistinct against a foggy background, while dawn in a faint, milky glimmer struggled to free itself from the thick dark of night.

Standing at the open window, our traveller seemed to be looking for auguries for his departure, which was imminent at last. The mist rising off the sea did not dismay him at all; in fact, from his observation point he strove to make out the black outline of the vessel on which he would shortly be embarking and, as if to make himself acquainted with his future home, he began to sort out the intricate muddle of masts and sail-enshrouded yard-arms. The chest containing his clothes, and the one with the less precious merchandise which he was sure of selling just by paying a visit to a few old friends in the Danish capital, were already stowed in his cabin on board. Nothing was left but a small leather bag containing his money and the picture in its wrappings. Propped up in its usual place, swathed and protected like a newborn baby hidden in blankets and swaddling clothes, the canvas seemed to be patiently biding its time.

Bernhard once again made sure there were no flaws in the

wrapping, lest the damp should get in and spoil the precious work, and that the cords were still tight. Then he went down to the dining-room. From the kitchen came the clatter of dishes, a sign that the maid was already busy with the master's breakfast. The sound of his chair scraping as he sat down at table spurred the woman to even greater haste, and a little while later, her face flushed from the fire, she appeared bearing a steaming dish.

"How did your mistress sleep, Annie?" asked Master Van Rijk, eyeing the dark bread placed beside the large slice of fragrant roasted meat.

"Badly, sir. She had a restless night full of forebodings." Bernhard clearly discerned the resentment and rancour in the old woman's words. "She'll not dare to tell you herself, sir, but you really ought not to leave today." Then she muttered something between her teeth, which her master was meant to hear only indistinctly, for the maid was not bold enough to speak her mind any further.

"Will she be coming down to breakfast?" Bernhard cut her short without taking too much notice of the tartness of her reply.

"I don't know if she'll come down or not. She's still tired and depressed. It's not good for a woman in her state, and at her age, not to sleep at nights."

"Tell your mistress not to leave her room. I'll come up and say goodbye. Off you go and tell her, then. I don't need you here any more."

He finished his meal in blessed solitude, without any further nagging, and in the meantime the day had grown lighter and clearer, although it showed no promise of being a bright, sunny one. He leant back in his chair and looked out towards the harbour, of which he could catch a glimpse through the window behind him. He pictured to himself how lively it must be becoming, with the bustling of sailors and cabin-boys. He had arranged with the captain to go aboard fairly early in the morning, when the vessel was ready to weigh anchor. He reckoned that he still had nearly two hours to make his final arrangements, to give another thought to his luggage in case he had forgotten anything, and to take his leave of Miryam, who was expecting him upstairs. He sat there a short while longer, dallying with his thoughts, then pushed back the chair and went straight up to his wife's bedroom.

He gave a light tap at the door and entered without waiting for a reply. Mistress Van Rijk must have been up for some time and was waiting, like an enthroned monarch, for her husband to pay homage. Attired to perfection, she was wearing the same yellow dress as on the previous evening, and in her hair she had woven the string of pearls her husband had given her on their wedding day. The pallor of the precious drops toned in with her luminous skin, as if the pearls themselves were part of her complexion.

The tranquil look with which she welcomed her husband reassured Master Bernhard, if such were still necessary, as he went over and seated himself opposite her beside the window which, like the one on the ground floor, gave on to the harbour.

"They tell me you didn't have a good night's rest, and I'm sorry to hear it. Even so, I can't see any weariness in your face. In fact, it's more radiant than ever."

"Go on now! Don't listen to women's chatter. Annie's been trying to intimidate you, hasn't she? She's nothing but an old fool, and thinks my pregnancy is going to cause all sorts of troubles, now that you're going away and leaving me alone."

"But you don't like my leaving either, Miryam . . ." The

merchant's gaze roamed around the room and then, unwittingly, returned to the rectangle of the closed window.

"Is that your ship? The one down there?" Miryam leant forward across the window sill.

"Yes, that's her; and there's only an hour, or perhaps a bit more, until she slips her moorings. The wind seems fair. At least for today we'll be sailing in perfect calm, and the sea is a pleasure to look at. We shall head up to the northern tip of Holland and there, once past the island of Texel, we'll strike the current. After that it will be easier. The captain is an excellent man – you know him yourself – and even if this passage is costing me more than usual, well, the valuable stuff I'm taking makes the expense worth while."

"I'm sure it does . . . even for me, waiting behind with an equally precious burden." And she smiled pleasantly.

Master Bernhard felt (how shall I say?) caught out by his wife's innocent reproach, and he guessed that Annie's strictures were not entirely the product of the old woman's fantasy. Nevertheless, he would leave without remorse. Seeing Miryam's fine profile he was once again struck by the purity of it, so regular as to elude a superficial glance. In spite of the veiled reproof of a moment before, he felt himself at that instant to be a man completely fulfilled. Rising from his chair, he approached his wife and stroked her hair, gently fondling the string of pearls woven into it. He was about to put his lips to her forehead when out of the corner of his eye he saw that the door was ajar. He gave a conspiratorial smile, quickly went across and closed it, and turned the key in the lock.

Shortly after eight o'clock on an overcast morning the imposing three-master weighed anchor and glided out to sea, leaving astern the harbour of Scheveningen. From the quayside they watched it move away, cumbersome and hesitant, its matronly dark outline rocking softly on the surface of the water as it made for the open sea, urged by a gentle breeze. It could be seen for a long time, in silhouette on the horizon and already far from the teeming harbour, until those on shore, thinking they could still make it out in the farthest distance, were in fact gazing at nothing but its phantom, retained in the mind's eye like a mirage.

Master Bernhard, on the upper deck, kept one eye on the sailors hurrying about their work and the other on the town as it slipped away, soon to be swallowed up in the unrelieved grey of the coastline.

It was a calm voyage from the start, and the vessel's course was never very far from the coast, which was visible from time to time as a light, misty outline.

Van Rijk was the only passenger on board, so that he spent many an hour alone in silence, leaning on the ship's side and following the regular, mysterious pulse of the waves breaking against the hull and shattering into greenish, iridescent spray. Rarely did he take his eyes off the chasing fluctuations of the waves against the ship's sides, and went so far as to pattern his thoughts on the monotonous rhythm of the waters. It was then that he thought of bringing Miryam a gift of a crystal bowl, with reflections resembling those lustres of the sea which so entranced him.

Sometimes, in the course of his stationary meditations, he was interrupted by the presence of the captain, a pleasant fellow with plenty to talk about. From the first day out the latter had paid unusual attention to his passenger, going much further than the usual ceremony of inviting him to his table. Despite the life he had led for years, almost always at sea aboard merchant ships, and in the company of coarse, uneducated men, he himself was anything but rough and rude. With Master Bernhard, moreover, he had discovered the pleasure of long, leisurely conversations, which he indulged in whenever the management of the vessel required no more than routine attention. In fact, he saw his guest as a man of some talent, or at least this is how he put it to himself, thinking back on one of their early talks.

It happened more and more often, at the end of the day when the evening breeze grew more penetrating, that the two men felt inclined for relaxation and, as a first step towards familiarity, allowed it to transpire from what they said that they would like to know each other better. It was usually up to the captain to take the initiative, but the other willingly followed his lead, and indeed supplied him with new topics when it seemed that the conversation was languishing or running aground due to excess of tact.

"Is it always so calm on this run, sir?" asked the merchant, one evening when the wind was blowing sluggishly and scarcely filling the sails.

"By no means. It's quite an exception for the weather to hold as mild as this, and for so long, even in the good season. They're treacherous seas and coasts, these. Anyway, you know them yourself."

"I've seldom sailed on this route, and then only part of it, years ago now. We were headed further north, towards Norway, and only saw the Danish coast in the distance. Later, when I had occasion to go to Copenhagen I thought it better to cross Germany and embark at Lübeck. In that way I could stop off and see a merchant in Hamburg."

"It's not long now before we leave Dutch waters. We're nearly abeam of the island of Ameland. If you look carefully over there, to the south, you'll make out the coastline. Another few miles and we'll sight the lighthouse."

[69]

The merchant strained his eyes into the gloom, which was not yet so very dense, for it was still tinged with the last rays of a slow sunset that lingered on interminably at their backs. He looked behind him too, struggling to glean the last of the evening light to shed upon the darkness which they were moving to meet. It was the hour at which the line between day and night becomes most clear-cut: to the west the sea was still silvery, and silvery also was the wake which the vessel left astern. But its bulky hull was moving towards the shadow crowding in from the east.

Master Bernhard was unable to make out anything beyond the restless play of the surrounding waves. Even the line of the horizon had vanished, but he went on staring into the dark, reassured by the invisible presence of dry land.

"You can't see it, am I right? It must be long experience of this run that has sharpened my sight. I believe that even if I went blind I would still be able to make out that strip of land," said the captain. "See the lighthouse over there?" He pointed, a little later, to a faint glimmer in the unremitting night that enclosed them on all sides.

"How many years have you been sailing these seas?"

"Over twenty years, sir. Strange that you should mention it, just as I am taking a vessel on this run for the last time."

"The last time?" cried the merchant, taken aback; but he received no reply whatever from his companion.

The wind had risen, and the cloaks of the two men lifted heavily and awkwardly in the strongest gusts, falling again at once with a muffled flapping sound.

"You, on the other hand . . . why have you taken to the seas? You don't seem to have brought much cargo."

"Why have I taken to the seas, you ask? Well, I do in fact have merchandise to sell, a friend to visit in Sjaelland, and

. . . Well, I'm a merchant, and every now and then I have to travel, either by sea or by land. I enjoy it."

"Very possibly, but this voyage is going to set you back a lot, and I doubt whether you'll get your money back. You deal in pictures and valuables, don't you?"

Van Rijk nodded, and felt a secret thrill of pleasure at the thought of the little package safely stowed in his cabin.

"Then why don't you think of trading with the Indies? Those are countries where you really strike it rich."

"And ought I to abandon my own wares for a reason like that?" smiled the merchant with a touch of pride. "Should I give up these treasures for a new stock-in-trade? No, no, certainly not! I have too much at stake in this business of mine. Just think if I were to lose it all out of curiosity or, for that matter, the riches of distant lands – and amongst such strange people!"

"There are lots of Europeans living out there now, and they're richer than the rich who stayed behind. Anyway, what do we know about the people of another world? Speaking for myself, I've decided to leave these seas. I know them too well and they have nothing more to give me."

Master Bernhard thought of the invisible profile of the coast of Ameland, but he said nothing.

"You don't know how much the ocean has to offer, my friend. Things that neither you nor I can imagine."

"With the result that you bequeath me the land of Denmark!" broke in the other merrily. "Your last voyage will be an auspicious one for me." Van Rijk's eyes were laughing in the darkness, so intense that it swallowed up even the pallid glimmer of the lighthouse on the island, the last vestige of Dutch soil. The vessel had in fact made a sort of sudden leap into the open sea, and for days on end there was no further sign of land.

*

Following that conversation in the dark the captain was taken
up with a host of chores that kept him constantly on the go, so
there was no chance of his talk with the merchant being resumed. The ship proceeded peacefully across the open sea,
alone. In fact they sighted only one ship. Eastward bound, it
was small, with a single, square, black sail; its diminutive
outline soon faded out on the horizon.

Van Rijk was not short of time for thinking, and his destination, now quite close, should have suggested food for
thought. The impetuous plans which had enlivened the days
before his departure seemed quiescent, resting in the depths
of his memory, drifting up from time to time like weightless
bodies. On the other hand he would lose himself in long,
meaningless meanderings, or in leisurely study of the precise, geometrical flight of seagulls round the ship, whose
numbers increased or diminished according to whether the
vessel was inshore or far out to sea. With a sense of wonder he
watched their dark forms outlined against the sunlight when,
on wings motionless for long seconds on end, they let themselves float on currents of air. And he too, our hard-headed
merchant, was suspended and motionless between air and
water, in the power of an energy that was not his own, which
bore him who knows where. The nature of the voyage, and
the fact that it was relatively short, should not have prompted
him to such reflections, but an unusual frame of mind ran
counter to the reality of things and upset them. He thought
very little about his house in Scheveningen, and he thought
little even about Miryam. Of her, it is true, he preserved
intact the pleasing harmony of colours in which she was
arrayed on the day of his departure, but he had trouble in
defining, between the yellow of her dress and the pallor of

the pearls, the fleeting lineaments of a face that was so familiar to him.

One evening during dinner the captain announced to his passenger that, if the wind kept constant, in three days' time they would drop anchor in Holbaek harbour.

"So we have arrived," said the merchant softly. The candlelight shone gold upon his face, and golden also appeared his eyes and the thick yellow moustache on his upper lip.

"Yes sir, we have, and I cannot remember a calmer voyage than this has been. Soon we'll be within sight of the Danish coast, and the approach is child's play. When a voyage is almost over I am in the habit of drinking a toast to the happy outcome – something I always do alone. On this occasion will you give me leave, in your company, to . . ."

"Are you not being rather hasty, sir? You said yourself that we still have three days to go: three days are long in passing, and anything may happen."

"Nothing more can happen at this point. You yourself, your precious cargo, my ship, we are all as safe as if we were already at our moorings. For my part, I would like to congratulate myself, and also to congratulate you."

"I deserve no credit whatever for the success of the voyage," rejoined the merchant, who was in fact pensive and withdrawn. He spoke unwillingly, in a low voice, while his gaze wandered hither and thither, shying away from the spirited vigour of his companion.

"You are of a singularly patient nature for a man of business. I have chanced in the past to take aboard other merchants, and to feel oppressed by their impatience to arrive. They are all in a hurry to have done with the suspense of travelling. You have had this experience yourself: one lives for days on end simply waiting for land to appear on the horizon."

"Suspense . . . you've put it well, my friend. Suspense
. . ." repeated the merchant, who had, however, passed over
the captain's last remark and was dwelling on that other
vague notion left hanging in the air.

"Well, Master Van Rijk, I am grateful to you for not wishing to jostle me with your haste. And yet, I recall that when
you came to negotiate your passage in Scheveningen you too
seemed anxious to reach Danish soil."

It fell once again to the captain to get over the embarrassment which, for no reason, had arisen between them. From a
locked cabinet he fetched out a dark bottle.

"Burgundy wine," he said. "The very best, for times like
this."

The merchant smiled, and held out his empty wine-glass
towards his host.

"As you wish, captain. We will drink to your health and my
patience."

"And to our safe arrival, now that we are within striking
distance," added the other. He began to sip slowly at the
wine, between whiles stealing glances at his table-compan-
ion. Just then, had it not been for the deceptive play of the
candles, now throwing long streaks of shadow, now shedding
light on the merchant's face, he could have sworn that he
caught a glimpse of some remote boredom in his eyes, some
strange and ill-concealed ennui.

"How old are you, sir?" he asked, pouring him out a second glass of wine. Whether on account of his own distraction,
or because in putting such a direct question the captain's
voice had dropped considerably, Van Rijk did not hear a
thing. He finished his wine sip by sip, replaced the glass on
the table, and remained for some moments in thought, his
fingertips gently stroking the white tablecloth and the stem
of his glass. Then, shaking himself out of his rapt state, he

rose from the table, made his excuses to his host, and took his leave. He went below-decks and turned in early. There in the dark he pondered on many things, until the confusion of first sleep came to mix his thoughts with far-off memories, in a jumble of fantasies that had nothing to do with the seriousness of a grown man.

Before consciousness surrendered altogether, clear and distinct within him he heard the captain's voice: "How old are you, sir?"

Three days passed after that evening, and as the captain had predicted the Dutch merchantman sailed into Holbaek harbour.

To Master Bernhard the place appeared desolate and inhospitable, and he felt a pang of regret at having to leave the ship and confront a country of such unprepossessing aspect. He went below, shoving his way through the crew already at work unloading the cargo, and reached his cabin. He closed the door and carefully gathered up the little bag which he had kept beside him throughout the voyage. The rest of his merchandise was ready to be unloaded and stored in one of the port warehouses, where it would remain in deposit until he had planned his itinerary in Denmark. Up on deck again, he spotted the captain busy with the unloading. He thought of approaching him, but held back and made for the gangway, wedging himself into the jostling stream of men and materials, among which he recognized his own crates as they were laboriously borne ashore. Turning to give a last look at the deck of the vessel, he met the captain's eyes, apparently fixed upon him. The two men bade each other farewell from a distance, with brief nods, then Van Rijk moved away from the ship to make arrangements for his goods.

He had scarcely started along the quayside when he was approached by a tall, fair-complexioned youth who garbled his name in an anxious, enquiring tone of voice. He proffered a neatly folded letter on which a familiar hand had written: Master Van Rijk of Scheveningen. This, with reluctance and hesitation, he gave to the merchant. The note came from the Danish nobleman, informing him that the young man standing before him would escort him by carriage to the house, where he was expected. The letter was dated 24 June, which meant that the messenger had been waiting two days at the dockside for the Dutch ship to arrive. Bernhard glanced at the young man, who for his part continued to observe him with misgiving.

"I am Bernhard Van Rijk of Scheveningen," he said at last. "You have been sent by the lord of Herfølge to take me to his house, have you not?"

Of these words, though delivered with studied slowness, the blond youngster grasped only the two names, but side by side they reassured him that he had not been mistaken in his man. He thereupon tried to explain as best he could that the gentleman's bulky luggage could also be transported to the house, and to this effect he pointed first at the crates and then turned towards a simple wagon by one of the dockside warehouses. The hefty youngster wished to help his master's guest in some way, but the sailors shoved him aside as they hoisted the crates on their shoulders, fearing that they might have to share the tip with him. Van Rijk also, though more politely, declined to let him carry his small bag as they walked towards the cart. He saw to it that the crates were carefully stacked, checked that they were firm, and dismissed the sailors with a handful of small coins. Then he climbed up on to the box next to the young man, because the rest of the space was taken up with luggage.

Both Van Rijk and his companion had abandoned any attempt at conversation. To the merchant, not knowing where they were going or how far they had to travel, the journey seemed long and uncomfortable. From time to time he stole a glance at the lad beside him, attempting to decipher . . . exactly what, even he would have been unable to say; and the latter replied with a swift, untroubled look and went back to watching the road ahead.

They had left the sea at their backs and were making their way into a landscape of intense colours, shining as after a storm. The cart-track followed the capricious line of the hills which rose up ceaselessly one after the other. They were modest knolls, but frequent, such as Bernhard had never seen before, and his gaze, accustomed to resting on unbroken plains, was wearied by the nervous heaving of that endless undulation. Even the colours seemed to him exaggerated, charged with powerful, aggressive dynamism. Meanwhile the wagon, with a few hard bumps on the way, had left the yellowing fields of oats and turned towards a wood. All scent of the sea was lost and, although they had trotted only a few miles, to Van Rijk it seemed as though they were penetrating the heart of a vast, silent, uninhabited continent. He began to tire of looking, and tire even more of the irregular jolting of the cart. He would have liked to ask for a rest, except that his escort showed not the least sign of fatigue, while the horses had just started to cut a brisker pace, as if to let one know that they were not far from home. A moment later, in fact, the lad stretched out an arm and pointed to something which Van Rijk could not yet see. Suddenly they took a right turn into a narrower lane, and then the merchant caught a glimpse of the reddish bulk and square outline of a castle.

They skirted a huge, well-kept garden, the dense greenery of which sheltered a large building visible only from time to time through the foliage. Only after yet another right turn did the castle come unexpectedly into full view. Spanning a moat, a stone bridge led to the wide aperture of the main doors, with a grey stone archway standing out in relief against the deep red grandeur of the façade. But however vast and solemn the castle was in appearance, enveloped in a species of aristocratic silence, from close to it had an invitingly domestic air to it. The courtyard in which the wagon drew up was a small quadrangle overlooked by a great number of windows, but at none of them did Bernhard see a face peering out, alerted by the clatter of hoofs and the rumble of wheels. The young man had leapt briskly to the ground and held out a hand to the guest, who hurriedly clambered down, giving a tug to his cloak, which had snagged on a corner of the seat; then he looked enquiringly at his guide. With a deferential gesture the latter indicated a small, closed door to his left, and preceded Van Rijk up the three steps and into a dim hallway. Light came from a large window at the far end of a corridor, looking out on to the trees of the park and affording a tenuous, greenish luminosity.

The room into which the merchant was shown was filled with the same light, for the three windows, facing on to the garden, gave a view over extensive lawns with grass of a tender, newborn greenness. Approaching these windows, Master Bernhard saw before him the moat, with lawns sloping down towards it, and beyond the water the walks and paths leading into the thick of the trees. Right on the bank, crouching with its muzzle on its forepaws, was a sheepdog, waiting motionless.

"What a magnificent creature," thought Bernhard, and imagined seeing it rise to its feet at a signal from him; but a faint rustling of clothes behind him brought the merchant's attention back into the room. Standing near the door, a woman of about forty, dressed in grey with sober elegance, was waiting to address him. Her face was serious, and she had a fair complexion like that of the young servant; her white lace collar was the only softening feature in an almost nunlike appearance. Bernhard bowed, embarrassed by not being able to determine the status of the woman, whether she was the housekeeper or his hostess in person.

"Welcome, Master Van Rijk. The lord of Herfølge has asked me to receive you in his name and show you to your room."

"His lordship is not at home, then?"

"He has gone down to the village with the young lady his daughter, and will return in a few hours' time. In the meantime, should you require anything, I am at your disposal and will see to it."

What the woman thought she discerned in Van Rijk at that moment – pique at not being received by his host – was in reality no more than embarrassment.

"Madam, I . . ." he started to say, but he was immediately interrupted.

"Excuse me sir, I will lead the way. The servants have already taken up your luggage." And she set off for the staircase leading to the bedroom floor. Van Rijk followed meekly, subdued by the stern regality of the woman, who mounted the stairs before him with unexpected grace and lightness, despite the fact that her movements were controlled to her very fingertips. She stopped at a heavy door, opened it, and stepped aside for the guest to enter. The room was spacious, with a large bed recently made up (one could still see the fresh creases in the sheets), while a door in the wall opposite the bed gave into a smaller study. There Master Bernhard's

[79]

luggage had already been laid out in scrupulous order.

"Should you wish for anything, or need my help, do not hesitate to call," said the woman, indicating the bell-rope. "And now, if I can be of no further assistance, with your permission I will retire."

Left on his own, Bernhard began to inspect the room, which was sparsely furnished but by no means bare. He paced restlessly from one corner to another, unable to still either his mind or his eyes, as he continued to pry around. Finally he returned to looking out of the window, which faced on to the west side of the garden. Beneath him was the moat, crossed by a little wooden bridge, beyond which began a broad walk of beaten earth, completely deserted.

He did not think of his luggage until some time later, and started by picking up the precious package, which he himself had left on the ground, and placing it on the bed. His hands shook with the effort of controlling his haste, and made him fumble the knots.

The painting seemed to him more muted than he thought he remembered: it had the colours of the Dutch countryside, and brought the memory of them flooding back, after the disorientation of the voyage had dimmed them. He told himself that that very evening he would ask his host's leave to retire early to his room, and at last send news of himself to his wife. The picture was lying on the bed, and the arrogant afternoon light was playing on it with sinister malevolence, seeming to Van Rijk to reveal in it a melancholy pallor which for all that time, in the muted light of his room in Holland, he had not been aware of.

For the first time, after all those days at sea, he was now on dry land, and the voyage seemed to him like a single endless day, with no incidents other than alternate sleeping and waking; and also without incident had been his arrival at the house of his Danish host. He thought it better to postpone his letter to Miryam for another day: he really had nothing to tell her.

Getting his boots off cost Van Rijk a great deal of effort and discomfort. He also removed his jacket and loosened his collar, for he felt a cold, sticky sweat on his skin. The silence which hovered round him, rather than calming him, made him feel nervous: even a footstep would have sounded dire in the deep stillness of the house, and Bernhard did not cease to strain his ears, in suspense. He was on a bed of thorns (though his generous host had not been sparing in comforts for him), but none the less he felt rising within him the most irresistible sleepiness, which he fought down, hoping against hope. Before yielding to another and even more ruthless attack of lassitude, he pulled himself together and glanced around him: the room was overflowing with light, and the canvas was propped against the leg of the chair, hastily wrapped up again, but not well enough to hide it from prying eyes.

"No one's going to come in here anyway," thought the merchant, his brain already fuddled.

What he thought to be only a passing drowsiness turned out to be a deep, way-weary slumber of several hours. He was shaken out of it by the sound, far distant at first, but gradually nearer and more insistent, of a faint knocking at the door. He blurted out an answer. Sitting up in bed, he could scarcely believe that the outlines of the room were dim in the half-light of an evening which entered dankly through the wide-open window.

"At your convenience, sir, my master is waiting. He has sent to ask if you are all right." The housekeeper's voice, severe and neutral, seemed to him unreal, and he had to gather every ounce of concentration to take it in. He answered breathlessly that he would be ready at once, just time to . . .

"At your convenience, sir." The woman's footsteps died away down the corridor.

Then he did not know where he could find a lamp, and he had trouble getting his bearings. This was not the moment to show discourtesy to his host, who must already have been waiting all too long. It sometimes happened to Bernhard, even in the most innocent circumstances (and these indeed were among them), to feel that he had been caught out or found wanting, like a child in the wrong, and the embarrassment he suffered on these occasions was considerable. He groped for his clothes in the dark, pulled on a boot, and in his nervous haste stubbed a bare toe on the frame of the picture. He remembered that the canvas was only half wrapped up, so he knelt down by the chair and, still groping, took it gingerly from the ground, spread out its dark protective cloth on the floor, and tried to wrap it and re-knot the cords, which he found nearby. At last he placed the package on the chair. He pulled on his other boot and opened the door. The corridor and the staircase were bright with the mellow light of candles.

When Van Rijk entered the drawing-room on the ground floor he found the lord of Herfølge alone, waiting for him, seated in a high-backed chair.

"Here you are, then." The affable smile which appeared on the face of the elderly gentleman made the merchant shy and ill at ease, and he tried to apologize for the regrettable lateness with which he had presented himself.

"You young need your sleep more than we old men do, and I ought not to have disturbed your rest. So you see that the fault is mine." Meanwhile his host was looking at him closely, friendly and unceremonious even in such formal courtesies. Then he invited him to be seated and asked him news of the voyage, of Holland, of his home and his wife. There was not so much as a mention of the reason for their meeting, of the picture which, in its rough wrappings, lay upstairs on a chair.

Van Rijk did not wish to subject his host to direct scrutiny; therefore as they spoke he looked about him, casting an eye over the furniture, and only from time to time glancing at the face of the old man who, having ceased to ask questions, was telling the newcomer how much and how anxiously he had been looking forward to his arrival. This was why he had taken the trouble to send a servant to the harbour to find out for certain when the ship was docking. He was sorry that, today of all days, pressing business had called him to the village, so that none of the family had been there to welcome their guest.

"I say none of the family, you notice; but the fact is that for years there have been only two of us, my daughter and myself. You will meet her shortly, at dinner," he added, interpreting a questioning glance from Van Rijk.

The latter, in the meantime, was attracted not so much by the words of his host, as by his hands: white and tapering, they revealed an old-fashioned elegance that enchanted Bernhard. So it was upon them that he dwelt, admiring them with the appreciative eye of an art dealer.

"As for the painting I have promised you, sir, I have it with me. But, well, I feel some misgivings about what I wrote to you, because now . . heaven knows what you will expect of my picture. I was certainly carried away when I described its wonders to you. So you see, sir, that perhaps I am not a good dealer. I realize that my judgement was too hasty." And he gave a sort of smile, as if to excuse and defend himself. Old Herfølge did not interrupt him, as one does not break in on someone giving vent to inner turmoil, but let him run on in the same tone of apology and apprehension, until it was Bernhard himself who stopped and looked at him, waiting for some reply.

"There will be time for all that, Master Bernhard. I am sure that you do not wish to hurry back to Scheveningen at once, since your wife still has quite some time to go. I would prefer that you should rest tomorrow as well, and after that we will think about business. One needs time and patience for everything, my friend . . . But I have not yet asked you if you like the rooms I put at your disposal. Are they comfortable, and sufficiently spacious? You will be staying for some time, will you not? So I would like you to feel at home in them."

Van Rijk was compelled to put his worries aside in order to follow what Herfølge was saying.

"Yes sir, they are ample and quiet. But I must confess to you that I am not accustomed to such silence. I live in a house on the main road to the harbour, and the dockside itself is very close by. All day long my ears are full of the sound of people shouting, the clatter of carts going to and fro, and . . . here one can hear nothing, not a voice, not a sound, and even your servants are so discreet one might think they were dumb! But the rooms, yes indeed, they are really beautiful, and I am most grateful to you, even though I am afraid I cannot stay long. I have to be in the capital soon, as I have some business to do there as well."

"We are very near the capital," replied his host. "But let us be on our way. Dinner will be ready and my daughter is waiting for us."

He got to his feet and started towards the door. Turning to

Bernhard, he bent an eagle eye on him. "Silence, sir, is one of the things I most appreciate."

In the adjoining room the table was laid, and the housekeeper was standing waiting beside a tall young woman with tiny, delicate features. The girl's fine, blonde hair was gathered at the nape of her neck, with escaping wisps at the temples that gave light to her face. She curtseyed to her father's guest, her movements revealing the same self-assured bearing that Van Rijk had noticed in the woman who first welcomed him to the house. During dinner the conversation continued quietly, the two ladies taking little part in it. The elder of them, seated next to the girl, played a slightly subordinate role, but her natural dignity led one to think that taking second place was the necessary homage paid to ancient formalities, and that far from being humiliating these in fact accentuated the woman's tranquil self-assurance.

At table they spent two pleasant, leisurely hours. Bernhard came to know his host better, and thoroughly enjoyed his company and conversation. So much so, that when dinner was over and the latter excused himself, saying that he wished to retire to the library, gently but firmly justifying himself by adding that the affection and familiarity with which he felt he could treat his friend enabled him not to forgo an old habit, Bernhard felt quite at a loss. He thought he would have been happy to go with him, but he dared not suggest this, and respectfully got to his feet when the elderly gentleman bade goodnight to himself and the two ladies.

Shortly afterwards our merchant did likewise and went up to his room. They had already lit the lamp, so he shaded it, and then stood at the window, watching the shadows stirred by the night wind in the garden.

*

Early next morning Bernhard and the lord of Herfølge met again in the dining-room, this time alone, the only other person present being a maid waiting at table.

"Did you sleep well, sir? I trust nothing disturbed you during the night?"

"Nothing, sir, except perhaps the wearisome discomfort of travel, which prevented me from falling asleep at once. I am beginning to think I no longer have the zest of a twenty-year-old."

"You are still young, my friend, and however tired you feel, you look healthy and vigorous enough to me. You are younger than I imagined. How old are you, in fact, Master Bernhard?" To ask this question he had leant confidentially towards the merchant and taken hold of his wrist.

"I shall shortly be thirty-four."

"There you see, I am right: I could be your father. Though I myself have a daughter who is still very young, too young for my years, and without anyone to care for her, apart from myself." He grew thoughtful, then released the merchant's wrist and leant back in his chair.

In the short silence that followed, Bernhard thought he perceived an involuntary rush of emotion, some deep, prophetic sorrow.

"If you are not too tired," said the lord of the manor, "perhaps you would like to come with me on my rounds of the estate. I make this inspection every morning, usually on foot, as I am not pressed for time. But, should you prefer it, we could take the gig."

Van Rijk happily accepted the invitation, but insisted that his host should do nothing to alter his routine.

A short while later they crossed the stone bridge and started into the wood, in the opposite direction to the one in which the merchant had arrived. Those few hours alone had sufficed for that countryside, so hostile the day before, to change complexion completely for the newcomer: not exactly friendly as yet, but becoming a little familiar. The morning was cool and clear, with a stiff breeze blowing, against which the two men stepped out vigorously.

"I am proud to be able to show you my estates, and at the best time of year, too. I'm sure you will get more pleasure from it on foot than you would riding in a gig." He was not the least out of breath, despite the brisk pace· he was keeping up with remarkable agility. The person who a short while before had seemed a placid, leisurely old man now revealed a hearty, youthful constitution toughened by constant exercise.

The same landscape seen on the journey from the harbour to the castle now lay spread before the merchant, and once more he marvelled at the haphazard undulation of the hills in contrast to the geometric discipline of the cultivated fields – a free-flowing yet orderly succession of lines and colours through which ran the hard, white road.

It was by this road that Van Rijk came upon the sea.

Nothing in the countryside around them gave warning of the beach on to which the two men emerged on leaving the wood. Before them glittered a deep, calm inlet that might have been a lake, but for the endless reach of the horizon that opened out beyond it.

"My land, as you see, ends here." Bernhard scarcely heard the voice of the companion at his side. He was astonished, for he would never have thought that the sea was so near the castle, which he had imagined to be in the midst of a far longer stretch of terrain. The old man laughed at Van Rijk's surprise: "Mine is a small country, as yours is, and one soon comes to the end of it."

They lingered for a while on the beach, and the sun was at

its height when they started back to the castle. For quite some time they walked in silence.

"Is it very long, sir, since you left your estates?" asked the merchant.

"I have never left them, Master Bernhard. Not even when I was young. I was born in the house where I now live, and have never slept a single night under another roof."

To the Dutchman this seemed an unbelievable thing, and he was overcome with a desire to put questions, but much as he wished to do so he was baulked by the utterly categorical nature of the lord of Herfølge's reply.

On re-entering the hall of the castle they found the young mistress awaiting them. Like her father, she behaved towards her guest with an openness such as Bernhard was not accustomed to; all the more so because her youth and inexperience, together with her meticulous upbringing, would have led one to expect a more reserved manner. Without the least sign of embarrassment she came up to her guest and removed the dusty cloak from his shoulders.

"Come, Master Bernhard," called the lord of Herfølge from the drawing-room, where he was waiting with a carafe of cool wine to hand. "Sit down and rest. Lunch will be served very soon."

In this manner that first day slipped peacefully by, as did the next, without any reference made to Van Rijk's picture. He was only too willing to let himself be swayed by his host's amiable disposition, and even when business once again summoned the latter into the village, his gift for making a visitor feel at home had already made it possible for Master Bernhard to find his way about unexpectedly easily. The brief period of time for which he was left alone was anything but wearisome. He was at leisure to stroll in the park and in the surroundings of the castle, and all on his own found the way that on the previous morning had led him to his discovery of the sea.

Retraced now without a guide this walk gave him special pleasure, and as he left that sequestered little beach he yearned for a chance to return there. But that evening he would be showing the painting to the lord of the manor, and thereafter, once the transaction was concluded, he would have no reason for staying on at the castle. He had been there for three days, and except in some distant haze he scarcely seemed to remember his first encounter with that demesne, with its silent inhabitants and his remarkable host. Furthermore, he still had to get to the capital, sell what little he had brought with him from the shop in Scheveningen, and make his way home.

With a pang of remorse he realized that he had not sent a single line to Miryam, but he comforted himself with the thought that everything at home was certainly running smoothly. Three days at the castle had evaporated, had been absorbed with such ease, that there had been no time to think of anything. At least, that was what the good Bernhard imagined.

He took a deep breath and slackened his pace: there was no reason to be in such a hurry. When he reached the stone bridge, instead of going into the house he turned to the right and wandered on into the garden.

The girl was sitting on a wooden bench under an elm-tree, and Van Rijk did not see her until he was just behind her and very close.

"Ah, is that you, sir?" she said, turning towards him with perfect self-possession, so that it fell to the good Bernhard to be caught unawares. But he recovered himself and replied with polished courtesy. The young mistress of Herfølge had a naturalness of manner that was most alluring, a strange halfway stage between childlike innocence and worldly-wise disenchantment.

He too sat down on the bench, looking with some apprehension at the enormous white dog stretched at the girl's feet. It was the one he had seen the first day, lying on the lawn beside the moat.

"He will do you no harm, sir," she said. "He may not look it, but he is a gentle creature." And with a bare foot she lightly stroked the dog's back, while it stretched itself luxuriously and raised its head to be caressed.

"My father tells me your wife is expecting a baby, and must be anxiously looking forward to your return."

"Miryam is a sensible woman with a strong constitution, and is certainly not having qualms about her lying-in. Besides, by that time I am certain to be home."

"How many children has she had?"

"This is the first. But, as I was saying, she is a strong woman, well used to my being away." (We have to admit that, in this particular case, Bernhard's memory was at fault.) "And then, the servants are thoroughly reliable. My wife is in good hands, and she knows it."

"This evening my father is going to examine the picture you brought with you," said the young woman, as she started to stroke the dog again.

"Do you know, madam, that I still do not know your name?"

"Ariadne."

Bernhard was surprised: "Not a very common name in your country, I think."

"You are right, it isn't. It was my mother's name, inherited from her grandmother, who was Greek. Or was it her great-grandmother, I forget. Anyway, it's an old family name, and my father wanted to give it to me."

The housekeeper was coming towards them down one of
the side-alleys, and her presence utterly put paid to the conversation. She had come to ask instructions from her mistress
about arrangements for lunch. It immediately transpired that
it would be more convenient to discuss this in the larder, so
they both took their leave of Bernhard and moved off and out
of the garden. Behind them trotted the dog.

Dinner that evening was rather earlier than usual, and when
it was over, without lingering at table, his lordship and his
guest withdrew to the library. It was the first time that
Bernhard had entered it at such a late hour, and the warmth
of the room, quiet and spacious in the golden candlelight, put
fresh heart into him.

"The moment has come, sir, to examine your precious
cargo," said the old man. The merchant somehow felt an
impulse to put that moment off, but the slightest hesitation
would have seemed insincere. He excused himself and went
to his room to fetch the painting, still wrapped in its black
cloth as on the first day.

When he re-entered the library he saw that an easel had
been set up in a particularly well-lit position: the choice of
spot revealed a thorough knowledge of the secrets of light
and shade, as well as a long-standing familiarity with the art of
painting. It gave the merchant a peculiar feeling of mingled
trust and trepidation, like that of a father consigning his only
son into the hands of the doctor.

The picture was small, and seemed lost against the vast-
ness of the easel. The lord of Herfølge rose from his chair,
drew nearer to the picture and gazed at it at length. How
often and how minutely had Bernhard imagined that scene!

But of all that he had planned to say at that moment, not a word was uttered. Neither of the two interrupted the other's different kind of silence. They stood some time, so close that their shoulders were almost touching. Bernhard saw that the black cloth, clumsily removed, had caught on one corner of the easel and was hanging there, but he dared not touch it until his host had stepped back and sat down again.

"Come over here, sir," said the old man at last, indicating a chair at his side, "and tell me where this painting comes from. You have told me nothing about the artist. I don't even know his name."

The two men talked for a long, long time that evening, and evening became deep night, and the light from the candles slowly waned until even the picture slipped into shadow. It was very late when Bernhard went to bed: not another soul was still astir in the house. The painting had been left in the library, enfolded once more in its black cloth and placed on the table. Nothing remained but to establish the price.

On parting the night before, they had agreed to let a day go by before settling that side of things, so that his lordship could examine the canvas again, at his leisure and by daylight. After that, Bernhard Van Rijk would be able to leave for the capital. Every Wednesday, moreover, Master Ør the castle farrier went into town with the wagon, and would be happy to take the guest with him, and help him to find lodgings for the brief time that he would still be on Danish soil.

That day, the eve of his departure, dragged on slowly for Bernhard. Impatiently, in oppressive, melancholy unrest, he counted the monotonous, featureless hours. The library door remained closed, and nothing was seen of the master of the house: not even at lunchtime, when the merchant had only the two women for company. Ariadne asked no questions about the previous evening, and made no reference to her father's absence.

"I hear that you are leaving tomorrow for the capital with Master Ør. Is that so, sir?" she asked, while the housekeeper was busy carving a large roast duck which the footman had placed on the table between the two of them.

"Yes, madam; and I hope that it is not too long a journey. In these last few days I have become unused to change and discomfort, and I confess that leaving your house will cost me some effort."

"Stay on, then," said the girl easily, but the housekeeper, though in her habitual respectful silence, made a slight gesture of vexation.

Such a natural manner once again embarrassed the Dutchman, though his departure did indeed upset him, as being nothing but a fruitless inconvenience. The picture had been disposed of in the best possible way, and as for the rest of the merchandise . . . well, it was not that essential to sell everything in Denmark. Were there no clients in Holland? So the days set aside for trading in Copenhagen could be better spent in the quiet of the woods, near the sea that fringed the lands of the lord of Herfølge.

Luckily for him Master Bernhard was sufficiently lucid to realize that this was only a fanciful daydream, and he replied to the invitation in the correct manner, with amused incredulity and a courteous refusal.

It was the lord of Herfølge himself who that evening, with generosity and even munificence, established the price for the painting, agreeing with the merchant that it was a gem of inestimable worth.

"The farrier will put off his departure for a few hours tomorrow, so that you may lunch once more with us, my friend. I am loath to see you go, and you leave me with the

[93]

fear of having deprived you of something precious to you, far beyond the value which we have set on it." While he was speaking the old man's eyes became clouded, and his voice seemed lustreless, revealing a crack in the polish which Bernhard had come to associate with him. He would have liked to reassure him that the work was certainly in the best of hands, that only because he had been confident of this had he journeyed all that way from his own country, and that he was proud to have entrusted it to the only person who, like an alter ego, would truly cherish it. But of all this he said nothing, confining himself to bidding his host goodnight, grasping the hands which the latter stretched out to him, and bowing until his forehead brushed them lightly.

Next morning Bernhard requested that Master Ør should not postpone the time of his departure. It was better for everyone not to disrupt the customary arrangements; and also, as far as he was concerned, it would be wiser to get to Copenhagen early, during the morning. No one begged him to stay on, his luggage was loaded on to the wagon, and once more Van Rijk took his place on the box beside the driver.

Once across the stone bridge, when they were bearing left, the merchant turned to take a last look at the vast bulk of the castle, until a hole in the road, or a stone, gave him such a jolt that he hastily scrambled to resettle himself on the seat from which he had nearly been thrown.

Four days later a Dutch ship sailed from Copenhagen harbour, taking Van Rijk back to his homeland.

Bernhard Van Rijk had no further occasion to return to Denmark. His business continued to flourish, and in it he carefully and profitably nurtured his only son, young Jan, who with attentive obedience imbibed his father's teaching, making the acquaintance of noblemen and merchants, both Dutch and foreign, and learning the correct mode of conducting business with them. Then he too began to travel the routes that led to the countries of the north, and also south, south towards Italy. He grew in every respect to resemble his father, with eyes full of that same restless curiosity which in his father was already showing signs of weariness, and the effect of the years; and he had the same jovial good spirits.

When our merchant died he left an heir worthy of himself, and the shop in Scheveningen continued to be the centre of a thriving web of connections in the art business, known to the most affluent families of half Europe.

It was on one February morning, near the end of his fortieth year, that Jan received a letter bearing a seal that meant next to nothing to him. It read:

Master Johannes Van Rijk, you will perhaps scarcely recall my name, whereas yours is well known to me. I should tell you that Master Bernhard, shortly before you were born, was a guest in my father's house, to which he brought a picture that I still consider the most precious of all the works we have collected over the years. Many years ago, when my father was near to death, he commended it to me with particular solicitude, and I myself am bound to it with the very same affection. It so happens that the events of recent times constrain me to be parted for ever from my house and all that is in it. But before this occurs, and while I still have authority over the properties of Herfølge, I should like the painting which we acquired from your father at least to return into your hands. I do not know whether, and to what extent, you are acquainted with the worth of the canvas: the subject is a woman's face

[95]

portrayed in three-quarter view; her head is enveloped in a turban, and she wears a pearl in her ear.

For a few months to come I shall be in possession of
the house, which is open to you whenever you may
wish to come, as it was to Master Bernhard your
father. I am confident that the affection which binds
you to his memory will make you prompt to accede to
my invitation.

With kindest regards,
Ariadne v. Herfølge

Prompt indeed was Jan Van Rijk in preparing for his first
journey to Denmark, following the sea-route which, after
leaving the coast of Holland, veers up to where the North Sea
meets the waters of the Kattegat, and then declines, island by
island, all the way to the Baltic.

THE LAST ASSIGNMENT

WHEN CHARLES V decided to leave Brussels and retire to the quiet of a monastery in the Estremadura, a place remote from the world, the very name of which sounded deathly and detestable to the few Flemish nobles called upon to follow the fortunes of their sovereign, the latter bethought himself of Don Luis Quisada.

Being the younger son of an ancient family from Valladolid, he enjoyed only modest resources; but the nobility of his birth constrained him to loyalty to the name of his house and to the emperor, dutifully served at court by Don Luis in his youth. Later on, chance and the whim of his master had banished him from a world which, all things considered, he had rather feared than yearned for. He was by nature impulsive and sincere, and was ill at ease among courtiers. Willingly he retired into the country at Valladolid, to preserve the dignity of his rank with all the effort which a meagre income entails in such cases. Shortly afterwards came his marriage to Magdalèn Ruiz, which removed the young Quisada from the court for ever. He returned there only once, to pay homage to the king and to present his bride.

In any case, the sovereign was the first to show that he understood the reasons for that retirement, and maybe it was in recognition of the hidalgo's merits that, rather than elevating him, he chose to lose sight of him altogether.

Yet, as he now made ready for his last journey, Charles wanted this man to be the first of his suite, the trusty, indispensable steward who would be at his side until his death.

Even before the *Bertandona*, the Biscayan vessel aboard which the emperor was to travel, had left the port of Flushing, the princess-regent of Valladolid sent a messenger to Don Luis, ordering him to be at the harbour of Laredo within ten days to welcome the guest who was returning, bereft of worldly titles and honours, to the land of his fathers.

At Don Luis's house they were not used to receiving royal messengers, let alone this one, who brought such unwelcome news! The master of the house went out to meet him in person, took the letter bearing the royal seal and read the laconic message. Joanna, princess-regent, adopted the same imperious tone as did her father, and Quisada felt himself foundering in time, plunging back at least twenty years into the past. On the 28th of September the emperor would be landing at Laredo. That was in ten days, exactly the time Joanna had allowed him to abandon everything and be on the spot.

But it was time enough and more for him to grieve, to look around him and lament the loss of his life of quiet, and to ponder upon the unfathomable ways of ironical destiny. Not for a moment did it enter his head to refuse.

On the morning of September the 25th he lingered in the yard of his house and watched the cart being loaded up with the few things he would be needing for his new life. The carter would be travelling by easy stages southwards to San Jerónimo de Yuste, while Don Luis had to hasten north to the Biscay coast, to be there before the ship dropped anchor. Our hidalgo set out before the sun was over the horizon.

Throughout the whole of that day he met no one. He had to press ahead post haste to the Cantabrian Sea, with the landscape stretching onward before him and the bluish line of the mountains still misty and distant on the horizon. He made a point of avoiding Burgos and carried on in solitude, deviating a mile or two from the straight line between Valladolid and Laredo. From out on the plain, to the left of the city, he glimpsed the isolated bulk of the cathedral soaring miraculously above the fields, as if there were no town surrounding it. Finally the mountains reared up before him, and the plains yielded to the first slopes of dark green foothills where the pinewoods thrived. He spent the night in an inn in Villardiego, at the foot of the Paramo de Masa, the pass which he must cross.

Our wayfarer's look of exhaustion, and the scanty baggage he had with him, did not give him the air of a man of consequence, so he was forced to accept a dilapidated straw mattress in a cubby-hole off the kitchen, the remainder of the inn having been booked up by a Biscayan gentleman travelling in the opposite direction. Don Luis did not complain about the accommodation, nor indeed so much as glance about him when the maid, carrying a candle, showed him to his bed, lifted the curtain separating his quarters from the kitchen, raised the light and moved it round in a circle so as to cast a brief, uncertain glimmer over the whole space. Then she lowered the light and went out.

"The light! Leave me the light!" cried Don Luis after the woman, who came back and lifted the limp partition again.

"Take a good look around you, sir," said she, once more turning the candle in a full circle. "I can't leave you the light because the landlord doesn't allow it. Anyway, in an hour or two the moon will be up, and give you all the light you need. Sleep well."

But Don Luis got no sleep all night. He tossed and turned unceasingly on his palliasse. There were moments when he thought his heart was growing calmer, that his thoughts were becoming free of the perpetual, insinuating phantoms that were plaguing him. But just as he was about to yield to exhaustion the same implacable apprehension caught at his throat, and once more he was in the grip of torment. Moonlight, as the maid had said, poured into his cubbyhole, throwing long restless shadows into which Luis peered wide-eyed, unable all the same to make things out more clearly.

Nothing in the world, he told himself over and over again, would make him trudge another mile, just to meet a stranger who lorded it over his life without compunction. On the morrow he would travel the same road backwards, and then his one and only serving-man would go to the palace and bring Joanna his master's refusal: with no explanation, just as without explanation he had been ordered to take to the road.

At the brink of dawn he dozed off, but was woken first thing in the morning when the bustle of customers dislodged him from his tiny corner. He asked for nothing but a glass of milk, then paid for his lodging and went out into the yard.

"Where are you heading for, sir?" demanded a powerful voice behind him. This must be the Biscay merchant, getting on the road at the same hour. "Are you by any chance going north, towards the Cantabrian Sea?"

Don Luis had not answered before the other went on: "Aha! You'll find everything astir up there. They say the emperor's coming back, bringing all those Flemish lords who wanted to have nothing to do with Spain." He laughed, not without a certain malicious relish. "And now they're on their way to be buried alive here! But what am I saying, calling it here? Buried in the middle of the mountains!"

He laughed again, with more relish than before. "You can't say no to the emperor, friend."

He did finally realize that the conversation was one-sided, so he stopped, remembered that another person was present, and said, "You haven't told me where you're headed for."

"Yes, yes, I'm bound for Laredo myself," replied the hidalgo.

"Then godspeed to you. Remember that in the mountains it's already cold. I crossed them yesterday. I admit it was nearly sunset, but let me tell you I couldn't wait to get down to the plain."

He rubbed his hands together energetically and began fussing over his gear, taking no further notice of Quisada, who meanwhile had moved over to his horse and was stroking its muzzle and feeling its warm tongue on the back of his hand.

Fifteen minutes later he left the inn and started towards the mountains. By sunset he should be at Villarcajo, almost over into the province of Santander.

The next few days left him not a moment of repose. Laredo appeared to be the epicentre of an earthquake and totally unprepared for it: Don Luis had to get to work at once to find lodgings for the imperial suite. He was assisted in this by the king's secretary, Don Gaztelu, who had himself arrived from Madrid only the day before. It was his duty to greet the emperor on the quayside, while to Don Luis fell the thankless task of arranging for the overland expedition to the

monastery in the Estremadura. Until the very day of departure, therefore, he had neither time nor opportunity to meet
the king.

The journey into the interior started a week later, and was
a venture that engaged everyone up to the hilt. There were
the good days, when the emperor was in as fine fettle as of
old, and there were those frequent spells of acute suffering in
which his gout made the slightest jolt an agony to him, pro-
voking yells of violent rage. Consequently the halts had to be
prolonged, despite the king's determination to reach Yuste
with all possible speed, while he had to be forced to obey a
doctor on whom he lavished all the cantankerousness of a
man not resigned to his malady.

Don Luis observed all this, day after day, though through a
sort of haze, and in the meantime continued unflaggingly to
smooth the route to Yuste. To achieve this he usually rode on
alone, a few miles ahead of the king's retinue, to arrange
things so that the discomforts of each stage could be kept to a
minimum. He was shrewd and efficient, so that the sovereign
in person, publicly and on more than one occasion, expressed
his gratification at having selected Quisada to organize this
journey. They passed through Burgos, Valladolid, Medina
del Campo and finally Tornavacas, the last village before
entering the valley of the Vera.

They reached the place on the 12th of November. It was
evening, and the torches burning along the street shed their
light on a dejected procession, shorn of any vestige of pomp,
on its way to a lodging scarcely suitable for such an illustrious
personage. Don Luis had been able to find no better.

Only when he had made sure that his master was being
taken care of in a well-heated room, at ease before a dinner of
august proportions such as the sovereign desired in spite of
the gout and doctor's orders, did Don Luis withdraw to his

room. Not two months had passed since the royal edict had summoned him to leave home, and already he seemed to have been on the road for years, while more years of trudgery stared him in the face.

"Any letters for Valladolid, sir?" The question was at that moment put to him by the messenger who would be leaving next morning for the north. Not for the first time Don Luis felt ashamed that he had found not a moment even to write a note.

"The best thing would be for you to go to my house and tell them that I'm well and that there's nothing to worry about." This he said to the messenger, and added, "Give me news of them when you return."

Alone in his room, he closed the solid wooden shutters and prepared for the night. He was the prisoner of a deathly weariness that not even a full night's rest would remedy. He huddled down under the covers, trying to shut out the din which rose from the room below. There, in fact, His Majesty was drinking toasts to the peace, to the serenity of his future dwelling-place, where he would cast aside the things of this world. A "Long Live the King" more ringing than usual burst through the ceiling and made Don Luis jump, as it pierced him in his first sleep like the stab of a stiletto. Yuste was now close by. On the morrow, after traversing Puerto Nuevo, they would come within sight of the plains, and the oak woods in which they had told him the monastery lay concealed.

"Don Luis! You must see to the loading of the mule-train. It is already daybreak!"

It was the voice of the secretary, Don Gaztelu, who was standing bolt upright at the foot of the bed and summoning him with all the persistence of a hangman. "His Majesty wishes to be at the monastery by this evening. We haven't much time, if you bear in mind that it's all uphill and the road is impassable! Did you know that the king's carriage won't be able to negotiate it? That's what the local peasants are saying. We've got to find a solution. So, are you awake now? Come on, my friend, bear up, or night will catch us in the mountains."

As things turned out, they reached the pass by midday. The first to arrive there was Don Luis, riding alone, and alone he looked down on the valley below. The autumn rains had watered the Vera well, and the valley was so verdant that it could have been the lushness of May. Far off he could pick out the unbroken mass of yellowing oak trees.

Don Quisada drew to one side to make way for the four peasants who came up at that moment, carrying the emperor perched uncomfortably on their shoulders in a sedan chair; and he made a bow in reply to a nod from his sovereign. Then, at the tail of the procession, he resumed his way downhill.

In this retreat at Yuste, the cell assigned to Don Luis (for it was no more than a cell) faced north, towards the oak woods which he had observed from the top of the ridge. The emperor's quarters were quite close by, overlooking the open sweep of the Vera and the gardens surrounding the monastery walls. This was the landscape which the king most cherished; although, from the second half of November on, the guests at Yuste could enjoy it only as a vague memory. Over the plain lay a thick, persistent fog.

In the monastery matins were said at the first light of dawn, or even before the faintest glint of day. The bell sounded muster with a note that itself seemed to be just emerging from the sluggishness of slumber, repeating stroke after stroke until it reached the most distant monk in the most distant cell. Then could be heard the scuttle of footsteps in the vaulted cloister, and then once more came silence, enfolded and swallowed up in darkness.

At the sound of the bell Quisada rose and opened the narrow shutter. Day after day the weather was the same: not a single shaft of light pierced the fog, and it was but the beginning of winter. Barefoot on the stone floor he moved across the dark room, avoiding the chair and the corners of the massive bed, and almost by touch alone found the clothes he had taken off the previous evening.

Compared with those of the monks, his footsteps resounded heavily on the cobblestones of the courtyard on his way to the main door of the Great Cloister and then, outside, in the lane leading down to Cuacos. In the warmth of the blankets on the rumpled bed abandoned by the hidalgo, the grey monastery cat curled up. It seemed to have selected Quisada for its master.

The latter was the only wayfarer, and had trouble in finding the path through the dense woods, even though daily for some time now he had travelled that route from the monastery to the village. One of his most onerous duties as steward was in fact to replenish the imperial larder every day, and though the most *recherché* delicacies sometimes came from very diverse and distant places, from Lisbon even, the local peasants had to keep up a constant supply at least of the basic necessities, which Don Luis examined and selected anew each time, before they were taken up to the monastery.

He was on his way through the wood when he thought he saw some hazy shape moving in front of him. He stopped, his hand on the dagger which he wore in the belt beneath his cloak. He was not even aware of a rustle of leaves, and could make out the path for no more than a yard or two before him. He was about to command this shadow to stand and reveal itself, but then he thought that no man, nor even an animal, would have been able to vanish so noiselessly. He stepped forward again, certain that he must have had one of those optical illusions which plague the imagination in the mist, and he chided himself for the panic that had made his blood run cold. Even so, hard as the going was, he realized that he had lengthened his stride in his eagerness to get out of the wood; and sure enough, in less time than usual he noticed that the trees were thinning out, and the milk-white light of a well-advanced dawn was spreading over the open spaces of the countryside.

Not far ahead of him a floating, lightfooted figure was walking swiftly in the middle of the path.

The hidalgo quickened his pace even more, drew abreast, and gave a rapid, searching, sidelong glance. It was a woman, more like a gypsy than a peasant woman. She was no longer very young, and her hair was long, dull with dirt and clammy with the damp mist. It was she who addressed him first, in an indifferent manner:

"Are you from the monastery, sir?"

Don Luis nodded.

"But you don't dress like the monks." She in turn gave him a sharp looking over.

"I am not a monk."

They went on side by side, the woman easily keeping up with Quisada's brisk pace.

"Ah, I see. You're a servant of the king who's shut up at Yuste." And she appeared to need no further explanation. In fact she ceased her scrutiny and drew towards the side of the path. In this way she had dismissed the hidalgo, who once more went on his way alone.

The lane led right into the heart of the village, where Quisada had his work cut out to steer a course between what people wanted to sell him and what he considered fit for the king. Above all he required fish, because His Majesty was very fond of it, whether lake-fish or river-fish, and it was not easy to come by among the meagre resources of Cuacos. At the end they offered him a bowl of milk warm from the cow, which he drank standing up, just before starting on the return journey. Then he shouldered a small keg of the same milk, to be brought to the king for his early-morning drink, leaving one of the peasants to load the mule with the rest of the provisions which, in a few hours' time, they would deliver to the monastery.

It was on his way back, and not far from where he had left her, that he saw the woman lying, a grey, forlorn heap on the sodden grass. Don Luis bent down and looked closely at her: she appeared not to be breathing. He grabbed her arm and gave it such a shake that he felt some of the milk from the keg slop over his back; meanwhile he lowered his face to hers. Her eyelids rose heavily, and her eyes held a look of bewilderment.

"Are you feeling ill? What happened?" he asked breathlessly, trying to think of a reason for such a collapse. "I'll help you to your feet."

And he got to his knees and grasped her under the arms.

"No sir, I am all right. I want to sleep, if you'll let go of me." With a faint, ironic smile she glanced down at Quisada's grasp, for very gently he had raised her almost to a sitting position, and was still bearing her weight. He laid her down again at once and she, without a thought for the man bending over her, or for his embarrassment, turned her back and fell asleep again like an animal.

When Don Luis re-entered the monastery it was broad

day, but the mist had not lifted and the light was faint and sluggish. He took his burden into the kitchen, saw to it that everything was prepared according to the orders received the night before, then went upstairs to supervise the king's awakening.

Gaztelu had got there before him, and was already deep in conversation with their master who, swathed in a heavy woollen cloak in an attempt to combat the cold and damp which the large fireplace made little headway against, was lying back in an unpretentious armchair, his feet up on a stool, listening to the secretary's daily report. Gaztelu, slowly and loudly, was reading the dispatches just received from Valladolid, so that the steward moved forward unnoticed. The room was still in a disorder that spoke of a night recently ended, the unmade bed, the clothing folded on a chair, and the air stale because of the unopened windows. Don Luis cleared off the table to make room for the dishes which the servants would be bringing in shortly, and his eye fell on some neatly stacked papers, written in the emperor's hand and broken off in mid-sentence. The writing was clear and easy to read, and the subject matter even clearer: it was a sort of memoir on which the sovereign was working, perhaps with the idea of passing down to posterity a more accurate account of his reign.

Quisada ran his eye quickly and enquiringly over a whole page, and did not raise his eyes until he had finished reading.

He then had to meet the gaze of the emperor, which had evidently been fixed upon him for some time, while in the room Don Gaztelu, in a painstaking voice and to no purpose, droned on, unconscious of how completely his master's attention was elsewhere. It was the footsteps of the manservant, arriving from the corridor with the breakfast dishes, that put an end to the embarrassment of that exchange of glances.

The steward laid the table for breakfast, paused to stoke up the fire, and left the room. A moment later Don Gaztelu broke off his reading to remind his master that it was time for him to take some nourishment, and helped him to the table where, awaiting him, was a steaming capon boiled in milk, sugar and spices.

As for Don Luis, who by nature was not inquisitive, once out of the room he would not have given a thought to anything beyond what little he had read. Deep down, however, he remembered the searching scrutiny of the king's eyes upon him. Days went by, and he thought he had forgotten all about the matter.

Every day throughout the winter he was burdened with the dawn journey to Cuacos, and the rigours of the season did not abate even at the end of December: they were worse, in fact, since misty days alternated with days of heavy, unremitting rain.

Christmas came, and the new year, welcomed and celebrated with all the solemnity which befits a religious community on these festive occasions; but on the king's part there was no lack of the profane ceremonial of rich banquets. Don Luis therefore went to no little trouble to ensure a regal welcome for the sovereign's few but illustrious guests.

Not until well on in the month, after St Antony's day, did the retreat at Yuste regain any peace and quiet, made necessary in any case by Charles's precarious state of health. For some time, indeed, the patient's attacks of gout had been more frequent, owing to the excesses in which he all too often indulged.

To the steward, sole wayfarer in the dark early hours of January mornings, the Vera began to seem less hostile. The winter damp and the frequent rains had prepared it for the verdant freshness of the coming season, and he fancied he could already discern the first signs of this, despite the abandoned state of the countryside.

One of the things Don Luis had grown accustomed to was meeting the gypsy woman nearly every day along the path. The two of them barely acknowledged each other, for there was really no reason why they should speak. In fact the hidalgo appeared to be scared of her. He could remember one morning just after Christmas, when he had seen her ahead of him, walking with that light, cat-like gait, and had slackened his pace so as not to catch up with her. It displeased him to recall that he had been so close to her that he still retained the mental image of the fine web of tiny wrinkles round her eyes and the deep furrow in her brow. He now regretted the impulse which had induced him to bend over her, and he regretted that absurd regret. He finally came to attribute it to the solitude of his life at the monastery, which caused his imagination to run riot. All the same, one morning at the end of January, when he found the woman waiting for him at the edge of the wood, and she wished him a happy new year, he could not help being touched by this belated greeting.

In February the weather grew more severe, returning to midwinter conditions. Beneath his feet the night-frost crackled, for with the end of the rains the cold had worsened, cutting through to the marrow. Don Luis had more than ever to push himself to quit his bed and face his daily trudge. At the start of the day he was still worn out from the day before, and his legs felt stiff and heavy.

One morning, while getting dressed, he even had to sit

down and get his breath back, but in spite of this he donned his cloak and went out: he was already late. In the cloister he met one of the scullery-lads, who stood aside to let him pass and gave him a puzzled look.

"Don Luis," said the boy in hushed tones, so as not to break the silence of the place. "What's the matter? Don't you feel well?"

"It's cold this morning, really hellish," was all the hidalgo said in reply, as if to himself, and having drawn back the bolt of the main door he slipped through without shutting it. The scullion hurried up to push it to behind Quisada, but not before he had noted the latter's slow, unsteady steps. His mouth hanging open, still drowsy with sleep himself, the lad looked out at the landscape lit by the first glimmers of day, and came to the conclusion that the cold was neither better nor worse than on the previous days. Don Luis was certainly not well: anyone could see that. He closed the door and set off for the kitchens, whistling under his breath.

Don Luis was indeed unwell. He walked haltingly, and it was not only the iciness that numbed his limbs. He made his way through the wood, emerging on the other side exhausted; and he still had to face the stretch of road into Cuacos, and the bargaining with the peasants, and finally the whole journey back to the monastery. He drew in deep breaths in an attempt to fight down the nausea rising from his stomach. He made what speed he could to the village, went so far as to be rude to two men who brought game for him to inspect, and simply could not wait to be home. At long last he started off with the little keg heavy on his back.

The gypsy woman came towards him from the wood, stopping a few paces away. Her arms were dark, firm and muscular, and she seemed to feel the winter's cold so little that she was not even wearing a shawl. Don Luis was relieved to see her.

"Good morning to you, sir." She scrutinized him keenly, tilting her head to one side and narrowing her eyes in puzzlement. Then she stepped up to him, slipped the straps of the keg from his shoulders without asking for a word of explanation, and casually shouldered the thing herself.

"I'm going your way this morning," she said. "I'm not in any hurry. Shall we start?" She had taken her place beside Quisada, and kept pace with his faltering steps.

"I shouldn't allow you to go to this trouble," the hidalgo objected without great conviction, and in the meanwhile he was walking side by side with the woman, impressed by the swing of her shoulders, which were scarcely bent beneath the weight. She was carrying it almost without effort, while he was having a hard time staying on his feet at all, and unthinkingly he laid a hand on her arm. Once out of the wood, there was the monastery quite close by, only a few hundred yards away.

"Please stop here. I can go on alone."

The gypsy woman unslung the keg and helped Quisada to settle it on his own shoulders.

"I have much to thank you for. Without you, I don't think I would have managed it." And he peered ahead with some misgiving at the distance he still had to travel.

The gypsy laughed. "You have nothing to thank me for, sir. Today it was your turn, and as you can see, I am in good health. Some other time, who knows?" She laughed again, and thought of the Samaritan who had bent over her in her sleep.

"Try to walk, it's not far. Don't waste time. Off you go!"

*

"I can do nothing more to help him. He may not even pull through." The emperor's physician had been urgently summoned to the bedside of Don Luis, who was lying unconscious, still wrapped in his black cloak. Only one bare arm protruded from it, bandaged at the place where they had opened a vein in an attempt to revive him.

"If one were to bleed him again . . . Don't you think it might help?" insisted Don Gaztelu, rather irritably. He too had been sent for, and at such an unearthly hour!

"Are you asking me to bleed him white?" answered the doctor with asperity, pointing to a bowl beside the bed, almost full of blackish blood. "I said I could do nothing for him. Someone must stay and keep an eye on him, and call me if need be. It would also be as well to send to Valladolid to inform his family of Don Luis's condition. He may never return home."

"Never return? . . . But, Mother of God! How can we tell the emperor? He will be most upset. In practical matters he trusts no one as he trusts Don Luis. Whom can we find to take his place, and here too, at such short notice?"

The doctor paid no attention to Don Gaztelu. He had gone to the bedside and once more felt the sick man's feeble pulse.

"Inflammation of the lungs is no small matter, even when it is treated in good time," he said.

Don Gaztelu made the excuse that no one had suspected it. Quisada had said nothing; in fact it was a miracle that they had realized even that night how serious his condition was.

"Take my advice: inform the emperor at once," repeated the doctor. "And the family as well!"

Before leaving the room he gave orders to a scullion to take away the basin of blood and his surgical instruments. He him-

self would make another visit, but the instruments could be
of no further use.

The secretary also left the room, making his way to
Charles's apartments with death in his heart. At Don Luis's
bedside there remained one monk, whose sole duty was to
watch the sick man lying motionless on the bed.

To all appearances Don Luis was resting. Of what went on
around him he comprehended nothing, and nothing did he
remember of what had happened to him. As a matter of fact
he had returned to the monastery, performed his morning
tasks in a sort of mental haze and then, without a bite to eat,
retired to his room. Still racked by the cold he had simply
muffled himself up in his cloak and lain down on the bed. His
head buzzed with a swarm of disconnected thoughts and a
babble of voices. More clamorous than any was the voice of
Don Gaztelu, uttering a string of names and numbers
vociferously but uselessly, since no one was listening. Meanwhile he saw himself dragging his limbs towards the wood,
with superhuman effort. Something sluggish drugged his
movements, and the more he tried to fight free of the en-
cumbrance, the tighter and more unyielding grew that overpowering grip. In one lucid moment he realized that he had
slithered to the edge of the bed, that his stomach was heaving
violently in spasms of vomit: then nothing.

He was found unconscious on the floor by a monk who,
from the room below, had heard the muffled thump of his
falling body, followed by a suspicious silence.

The emperor was deeply concerned, but not in the way
the secretary had feared. He thought it odd that no one had
noticed the steward's illness, and looked at poor Gaztelu as if
enquiring the reason for such negligence. But he did not wish
messengers to be sent to Valladolid: was there any real need
to rush things? He knew that his doctor was inclined to exag-

gerate, while Don Quisada, for his part, had a robust constitution. The secretary dared not contradict all this optimism, and hastened to obey the king when he gave orders that, to be on the safe side, his personal confessor Father Francisco should be dispatched to the sick man's bedside.

"Have you seen about replacing Don Luis for the duty at Cuacos?" was the sovereign's final question, and Don Gaztelu nodded vigorously, keeping his fingers crossed that he had made the right choice. Then he withdrew and the emperor, finding himself alone as never before at that time in the morning, quickly settled himself to his favourite occupation. He had his writing-desk and chair carried near the fire, and then got down to work, starting in at once from the last word he had written, without hesitation. He did have an excellent memory.

He also had great perception, or luck, in judging the destinies of men. Don Luis did not die.

It was a long ordeal that stretched ahead of him. Day after day, both around and within him, things were governed by a sort of lunar mutability, so that what awareness of life remained to him was subject to the same law of fluctuation as are the tides, now vigorous and aggressive, now unresisting, as when the waves recede. If that struggle between life and death left any trace at all in Don Luis's mind, it was that extraordinary intimacy which he, as a confirmed landlubber, was from then on to feel towards the sea.

When he came out of the coma he must have been disgusted by the state he was in, for even the monk in attendance on him had cause to complain of the patient's recalcitrant nature. This seemed all the stranger to those who had known the steady temperament of Don Luis before he fell ill. But this was only a lapse of a few days; Quisada thereafter, even in moments of the most acute suffering, regained the staunchness of character which everyone associated with him.

He left his bed for the first time two months later, so shaky on his feet that it needed two of them to help him to the chair, from which at last he could see outside, beyond the four walls of the cell. For two whole months he had not looked at anything, other than a dark stain on the white plaster of the room. Even then, it was not that he really looked at it, but he found himself turning his head that way at times when the pain in his back was at its worst, and it seemed that he could keep it within limits by taking up this position. This was an illusion soon dispelled, but he forced himself to stay still in that position all the same, for minutes on end, and he had made friends with that patch of wall. In any case, there was no other comfort for him on the walls: not a picture, not a sacred image.

He gazed through the window and yearned for the open air. He had really suffered, and was still suffering, from the squalor that sickness brings with it, the stifling smell of that stuffy room, and the stench of his own body. More than anything else he would have liked to wash.

A visit from Don Gaztelu occupied his thoughts for a moment or two. The secretary came assiduously, on orders from the emperor, to ask news of the convalescent, and occasionally stopped to have a few words with him, so as to have something reassuring to tell his master about the way the treatment was going.

"Don Luis," said Don Gaztelu that morning, "you need not hurry to take up your duties again. A rash step at this point would be quite unpardonable. I must say, though, that ever since the very first day His Majesty has been convinced that you would emerge from this unscathed. But now we must do nothing to anticipate your recovery. You are on the mend, aren't you? Very well, let's give it time and you'll be quite yourself again." He spoke in a suave, persuasive tone of voice, as was his wont with persons of exalted rank when he wanted to avoid some issue.

"My substitute has been satisfactory, so they tell me. The king will not have noticed my absence during these months."

"Satisfactory, yes of course. However, you understand, you are still indispensable here, and just as soon as you can . . . I don't say at once, but . . ."

"I wasn't asking to be released," Don Luis hastened to say. "That wasn't what I meant at all. In fact I think I could start again tomorrow, if only they'd allow me to get some fresh air! Then, I'm sure, I'd be better at once." And through the window he cast a look of restless yearning. Even so, just to shift in his chair he needed a helping hand from the secretary.

"Take it easy, my friend," said the latter. "You are hurrying things along too much. This climate has to be taken seriously. His Majesty made a strange choice in coming to live in these mountains, and between you and me, Don Luis, I don't like them one bit. Now I must get back to work. Look after yourself. It's not yet time to venture out of doors, so please remember that."

With this last warning Don Gaztelu took himself off, leaving our hidalgo alone and thoughtful. It seemed to him that the very next day he would have the strength to walk to Cuacos again.

Three more weeks elapsed before the doctor gave his *nulla osta*, after which Charles's consent was required, and Don Luis had to present himself to the king for a kind of final examination.

It was now well into the spring, and in the early afternoon the king loved to sit in the loggia which faced west towards the Vera. From there he overlooked the orchard, followed the sequence of the blossoming, and congratulated himself on the orderly exuberance with which his garden grew. The espaliers of pears were his greatest pride. He had the plants tended with the utmost care, knowing how delicate and demanding they were, and in autumn he wanted to see them laden with fruit. It was not that Charles was particularly fond of pears; what he liked most was the sense of opulence he obtained from the mere sight of them. In his heart of hearts he must have had great admiration for those Arab gardeners who were such masters at getting the most out of each plant, even in the desert. And Yuste, thanks be to God, was no desert!

He was therefore always in a good mood when he allowed himself this time of relaxation, the only one – despite his reasons for coming to live among the monks of San Jerónimo – in which he was altogether free from the world he had left behind him.

It was still something of an effort for Don Luis to climb up to the loggia, but he was rewarded by the tingling fresh air on the terrace, and he drew it deep into his lungs, no longer feeling any pains between his shoulder-blades. He presented himself to Charles, who was deep in an armchair among a host of cushions, and bowed his head respectfully.

"So, Don Luis, I am happy that I was not mistaken on your account."

"It was I, sire, who did not wish to fall down on my given word," replied Don Luis with a smile. "I owe you service and obedience to the end, and to the very end I will remain."

"Until the end of me: that's what you mean, eh, Don Luis?" And the king in his turn gave a laugh. "Quite right.

[118]

That's exactly what one asks of a trusted servant. Ah, Don Luis, I'm delighted that your illness has left you with this new spirit that enables us to consider even our infirmities with a tranquil mind. Sit down here and tell me if this part of the country isn't wonderful."

Quisada and his king were almost the same age, the latter being slightly older, though his corpulence made his features ponderous and aged him beyond his years. Those months in bed, on the other hand, had trimmed down the hidalgo's figure, while his pale face stood out with exceptional luminosity against the black of his costume. Seated beside the king, he too drank in the vivid greenness of the Vera: far off, to the south, one could just catch the silvery gleam of the Tagus.

"Not a single member of my retinue likes it. I know that very well. They only stay on out of obedience: obedience and duty. And fear." He raised his head in a gesture of pride, then continued with rather chilling levity: "My death, after all, will set the lot of them free. It will free you as well, Don Luis! Or do you wish to deny that this is how things are?"

"I did not take willingly to the task of accompanying you here. No indeed. It cost me a great deal to leave home." He spoke slowly, with some effort still, and long pauses to get his breath. "But it turns out that sickness has been a wise counsellor, and has silenced a lot of grudges. If I should happen to survive you, Your Majesty . . ." And he left the sentence unfinished.

"My friend, we understand each other better if we don't mince our words." There was no longer any trace of acrimony in the king's voice. "And now let's forget all that and talk about you. Don Gaztelu says that you are willing to resume your daily duties. You have no idea how relieved I am."

"I am perfectly certain that Your Majesty has been properly served in the meantime."

"They haven't done badly, I wouldn't say that. But you I trust as I trust myself, and I will not disguise the fact that your illness caused me some anxiety. Your wife, you should know, has only been told about it now that you are out of danger. It would not have been right to alarm her with such bad tidings. But to return to yourself, I was saying . . . yes, that you will rest for another two weeks, and after that you will do a little work here, without overstraining yourself."

"My duty in your household, sire, is the one you assigned to me from the very beginning. As you see, I am quite well now, and will not fail to carry out my duties at Cuacos as before."

They looked each other full in the face for a moment, and a strange gleam – sly, one might almost have said – betrayed itself fleetingly in the sovereign's eyes, bringing a slight blush to the hidalgo's cheeks, as if he had been caught out at some secret moment and was being urged into unwelcome complicity.

"One of these monks," began Charles, speaking slowly, "goes to Cuacos every day, and he is not managing too badly."

Don Luis looked out over the gardens. The silence rising from them instilled a kind of supernatural reverence, a feeling of awe far greater than that which the king inspired in his subject.

"It shall fall to you to render me a different service. You are aware, since you read a part one day, quite some time ago, that I am putting my memoirs in order. I don't trust what they are going to write about me. No one can know how or why I have acted as I have over years of government. It takes but a mere nothing to obliterate the truth. Very well, you have not lived at court, so you have no prejudices. You will be the first to read them, as I set them down. I don't want them to get into anyone else's hands until they are finished."

Don Luis nodded without giving a sign either of surprise or of any particular gratitude, and then took his leave of the emperor.

As if a great weight had been taken off his shoulders, Charles settled back into his cushions and let his eyes roam over the valley.

It was Martín Aguias who went every morning to Cuacos, and in order to perform this task he had the prior's dispensation from attending matins. Alone, following the path that led to the village, silently in his head or under his breath he would repeat the prayers which his brethren were intoning together in the church. No one interrupted his meditation, and indeed he himself permitted nothing to distract him. Thus for days on end he was not aware of being silently followed at some distance by a feline creature treading so lightly she seemed not to touch the ground, and vanishing before the houses of the village came into sight at the last bend, after the chestnut copse. And so things continued for quite a while.

Then, one morning, she was waiting for him. Crouched beside the path, she looked up at the monk as he passed close to her on his way back home with the keg on his back.

"Is it you who serves the king nowadays?" she asked him without beating about the bush.

"The king?" The monk had been taken by surprise, and gave her a mistrustful look. "Yes, I too serve the king, as we all do at the monastery."

The woman made an impatient gesture.

"I mean, you're the one who goes to Cuacos every day."

"Certainly it's I who . . . Don Luis was taken ill and can't perform this duty, so it's my job. But who are you?" He looked her up and down and softened a little. "You'd like to meet the emperor, is that it?"

"Heavens no! Why on earth? And for how long are you going to be performing this duty?" The woman was pressing.

"How long for? What a strange question! For ever, I imagine." And he settled the weight of the keg more comfortably on his shoulders.

Meanwhile the other had got to her feet, shaken the dust from her filthy skirt and set off, walking ahead of the monk, who was struck by the remarkable smell, a pungent smell of vinegar, which the woman's hair gave off as it glistened in the early-morning sun.

"Where are you going to at the moment?" he asked with some apprehension when they had already traversed most of the distance to the monastery. It had occurred to him that he ought not to have listened to her or answered, for the result was that he was taking her right to the very doors of the monastery, perhaps to beg, and this might be distasteful to their illustrious guest.

"Well then, where *are* you going?" insisted poor Martín in exasperation. No reply. Meanwhile they had left the wood and the wall of Yuste was already in sight. The woman halted and let the monk overtake her. He turned round suspiciously several times to see if she was following. The last time he looked back there was no one in sight. He entered the main door and shut it with care.

Once in the kitchens he urged everyone, with fractious insistence, not to leave the entrance to the monastery unlocked or unguarded. He made such a fuss that it was eventually pointed out to him that there was no reason for worry: the door was kept locked, and only those with business outside possessed the key.

But this was not enough to reassure him, and in the next few days the fears of the good Aguias became a sort of joke in the monastery; it soon passed round the servants like a new catchword, but no one seriously asked him what it was all about. He had become a figure of importance, that was the truth of it, they said; with the result that he felt threatened by everyone. The fact was, though, that every single day he met the woman . . . Not that she asked many more questions, but she was always there, as if she wanted to pry.

In the end he confided in Don Luis, who in the meantime had partly resumed the running of the king's affairs in the monastery. Who would be more likely to know something about it than he, who had gone that way so often?

Don Luis listened attentively to the monk as he told him his fears and asked for advice.

"But how can you be afraid of a woman?" he asked when the other had finished. "Going by what you tell me, for how long might she have come here begging? And yet she has never come near the place. Leave her alone: she won't do anyone any harm, or even think of doing so." And he went off, bringing the conversation to an abrupt close. But then he retraced his steps, as if having second thoughts. "Listen," he said, "I speak only for your own peace of mind: let me know if you happen to meet her again in the next few days. Though maybe she'll go away and you'll see nothing more of her. You say she's a gypsy, so she'll be moving on."

The steward's tone sounded to the monk as though he were scoffing at his fears, which he considered no less well-founded for all that. He shook his head bitterly and thought that he would have to look out for himself alone, and arm himself against the incredulity of others.

Quisada in the meantime had recovered almost completely, but there was no mention of entrusting him with the Cuacos job again. Since his illness his function had been entirely modified, transformed and elevated. He was more often present at the emperor's side than was Don Gaztelu, and though he had no hand in matters of government (news of which arrived daily at Yuste), he followed the drafting of the king's memoirs step by step.

But Don Luis was no longer the same man. Although the status to which he had risen was considerable, and his daily duties were lighter, since most of his former assignments had been taken over by the monks, his mood did not seem to derive any benefit from it. Indeed, he was often morose and taciturn. He felt Charles's good opinion, tyrannical and jealous, weigh heavy on him, and the hours spent in the western loggia seemed to drag by. The king dismissed him time and time again with the renewed obligation to be with him early the next day, as soon as he woke, because the mornings were devoted to the work of writing, which he had taken to with extraordinary zeal. He spent the first hours of the day on it, feeling that his mind was then fresh and supple enough to aid his memory. He referred with absolute precision to past episodes he himself thought he had forgotten, and which now seemed to him essential. Irrelevant details grew vast before his eyes, concealing motives and secret strategies, leading to still further enquiries, still further memories, in a spider's web that grew larger and larger, though to the old king it appeared more and more incomplete. Seated at his side, Quisada took notes with all the exactitude of total indifference.

When he retired in the evening to the solitude of his cell, he felt the vexation of another day of his life handed to the king and stolen from himself. This generosity began to be an even worse burden on him than leaving home had been in the first place.

It also became clear to him that he was not the only one to suffer: Martín Aguias had not overcome his fears about that strange creature with neither name nor destination.

One morning early, at the hour he had been accustomed to wake during the first period of his life at Yuste, Don Luis left his bed. He took off his night garments and, notwithstanding the dampness of dawn still seeping into the room, he had a long, thorough wash, shivering from the chill of the water from the jug. Seated on the windowsill, the cat gave every appearance of presiding with regal dignity over the awakening of her master. The latter then dressed with care, opened the door and delayed a moment or two before closing it behind him. The cat had curled up again, refusing the chance to leave the room, and Don Luis went down alone into the cloister.

The matins-bell was ringing at the moment the hidalgo and Aguias came face to face at the monastery door. The authoritative tone of Quisada's voice was enough to stifle the monk's surprise and caution, but he handed over the key with the fear of being an accomplice in some grave deed: so much so that, when he retraced his steps, he dared not show his face in the church for prayers.

Outside the monastery walls the Vera lay green and glittering with gossamer, lucent with the frost now dissolving in the sun, while in the clover-cups hung liquid pearly drops. His brow furrowed in a frown, Don Luis set out for the path to Cuacos.

Our hidalgo was accustomed to calling a spade a spade, and

since he had sworn loyalty to the king and, even more, promised it to himself in the depths of his being, what he was about to do was, in its way, a betrayal and a desertion. A battlefield, a council meeting, or the table to which Charles summoned him to record his memoirs: all these had equal value in the upright conscience of Quisada. Yet he did not turn back. He made his way into the thick of the trees and along the path like someone determined to reach a goal without delay.

He saw her crouching on the grass, motionless, her skirt tucked under the soles of her feet. She made no movement even when she heard the hidalgo approaching, and her shining eyes alone would have betrayed her had she not kept them fixed on the ground, riveted on the dew-damp boots that were trampling the hem of her garment.

Don Luis returned to Yuste at noon. Without anyone even hinting at the transgression he had committed, he read it in the eyes of the servants and, along with the reproof, he discerned curiosity about what lengths the king's fury might go to.

Don Gaztelu came in, and with all the rigid formality of a ceremonial asked him to hand over the key he had wrested from Martín Aguias.

"You will have no further duties for today," he added. "It would be advisable for you to remain in your room. The king will be sending for you at any moment."

The secretary himself would have given a lot to know what lay behind the conduct of this man on the brink of disgrace, but he dared not question him. Don Luis gave him the key without a word of comment or justification, turning instead to Martín Aguias, who had been made to accompany Gaztelu against his will.

"I beg you to forgive me for my insolence of this morning,

and to believe that it was not my intention to cause you to fail in your duty."

The monk heard him out with some embarrassment.

"Well, Don Luis, whatever you say . . . I don't really understand, but I'll certainly go on with . . ."

"Tomorrow in the village," the hidalgo broke in curtly, "remember to take care they don't skimp on fish, and make sure it's really fresh." He gave the two men a nod and retired to his room.

As soon as he opened the door the cat jumped off the bed and came to him; then it leapt on to the sill. Quisada opened the window wide and sat down in the light by the opening, his eyes closed and his chin on his hand.

He was aware of nothing at all beyond the comfort of the sun and of the silence. In his veins, dilated and calm as the sweeping reaches of the Tagus, the blood flowed placid and appeased. He thought, but without the slightest trepidation, of how the order which had ruled his life for years was now in ruins. He reached out a hand and stroked the cat, gently pinching it under the chin and tickling the soft down on its belly.

At any moment, according to Gaztelu, the emperor would be sending for him. In the meantime he watched the sun sparkle on the oak wood, his heart quiescent and grateful for each further moment of solitude that was granted him. He savoured the moments, he measured them with the careful parsimony of a jeweller weighing out gold dust. He had always thought of life as a gradual accumulation of years, and was astonished now to find how the tissue of time passed by more sluggishly, unravelling infinitely slowly, thread after thread, not so much hour by hour as minute by minute.

The cat, scratching and mewing at the door, distracted his

thoughts. He got up to let it out and returned at once to the window.

Later he watched the wood grow sombre in the shadow of a storm-cloud and the first fat drops of water mark the windowsill. Very soon the rain was hammering violently on the darkened, streaming stone. It slackened off little by little, but lasted until sunset.

No one came to summon Don Luis.

In the other wing of the monastery His Imperial Majesty was also watching the rain falling in the garden, angrily flexing his arm, where the gout had been worst these last few hours. His head felt heavy, racked with lancing pains. For this reason he had put off meeting Quisada, and was now scanning the fury of the storm in the hope that it would somehow relieve him of the stabbing pains in his head. Breathing heavily, he waited, but still the pounding in his head, those inexplicable shudders, that strangled feeling, left him exasperated. The storm passed, and the evening air with its returning clarity brought no relief to the sick man. These were in fact, all too obviously, the symptoms of the tertian fever that had gained an easy hold on his debilitated body, and that now raged, violent and implacable.

They almost had to manhandle the king to persuade him to lie down, at the anxious insistence of the doctor, from whom he none the less extorted a promise that he would be sent to bed for a few hours only. He had no time to waste on useless cures. Charles fell into a doze which was not a real sleep, and never recovered.

This was the beginning of the long month of the emperor's death agony.

*

The entire monastery participated in the decline of its guest, and in every heart there was a mixture of respect for his personage and wonderment in the face of an extraordinary event: Charles V was dying. But as it was not in his nature to give up without a fight, everyone present at Yuste had time and opportunity to contemplate what a death agony really and truly meant.

Naturally enough, no one gave any further thought to the fact that the steward had fallen into disgrace. They all knew with what discipline and authority he had for nearly a year ministered to his master's needs, and at this point all the tasks he had been relieved of fell to his lot again. He had to make the trip to Cuacos every day, and act more painstakingly than ever, since the provisions had to pass the strictest scrutiny, while he was forced to keep pace with the breakneck speed of the doctor's efforts to check the advance of the disease, which manifested itself in a ferocious fever. They were days of anxiety, days of uncertainty, but Don Luis did not lose his staunchness of mind.

He set out each day at dawn, and each day the gypsy woman was at the edge of the wood near the monastery. She walked with him as far as the fields surrounding Cuacos and there, on the edge of a recently mown meadow, she sat down and waited to return with him along the same stretch of road. They spoke little and barely even touched each other. It was at that time that Don Luis learnt from the woman that she lived a few miles beyond the wood, southwards towards the river. He did not think to ask her how, or with whom.

For some days the king's condition settled into periods of restless lucidity alternating with semi-consciousness. As the end was now very close, during one of his flashes of clear thinking Charles was asked if he wished to confess and take the sacrament. It was the steward's duty to be beside him at

the moment of communion, and to make sure that no frag-
ment of the consecrated host remained in the sick man's
mouth. He was bending over him when the king opened his
eyes, leaden with fever. Their gaze met for an instant, then
Charles relapsed into torpor. Quisada drew back from the
bed and left the room. Outside, Don Gaztelu, red in the face
from the heat and the exertions of those enervating days, was
waiting in trepidation.

"It's a question of hours, don't you agree?" He spoke in a
reverent whisper that irritated the steward, who thought it a
piece of ridiculous toadying.

"Hours . . . How can we tell, my dear sir? When it's time
. . . we can but wait."

The gypsy woman, on the other hand, never asked news of
the king, although she realized that the days at Yuste were
numbered. Summer was at its fiercest, the heat spread the
dense vapours of the river all over the plain of the Vera, and
the sultry air lent ponderousness to motion and to thought.
The king would soon have no further defence against death.

It was in the last hours of the night, a quiet, clear night, that
he passed away.

The bustle which followed the suspense of this death
involved every corner of the monastery, and a sort of ragged
procession moved towards the king's chamber. Two monks,
the two who had been present at Charles's last moments,
were kneeling in prayer, heedless of the low, agitated chatter.
Quisada also entered: and he was among the last.

From his cell he had heard at once that the king was dead,
yet he had stayed there, shut in alone, his mind empty of
thoughts. Looking now at those bloodless features marked
by the struggle borne for so long, he was aware of a distressing
dizziness: that face, far from being at peace, bore the signs of
an inconsolable nostalgia for life, as if in the teeth of death it

still sensed the vigorous current of time. Don Luis started at this insane idea, like one waking with a jerk from sleep. In a corner lay the package containing the memoirs of Charles V. The two monks were still praying, their faces buried in their hands. Don Luis approached the bed, knelt down, and kissed the silver crucifix which the king appeared to be grasping tightly. Then he crossed to the table, picked up the manuscript and left the room.

The funeral rites were long and involved, and Don Luis, an iron, intransigent master of ceremonies, organized them down to the most minute detail. Even Don Gaztelu had stepped aside before the authority which the steward now assumed in this, the last of his labours. Nine days after the king's death Yuste returned to calm and silence. All the courtiers were dismissed, the servants were paid off, and arrangements were made about Charles's bequest to the monks of San Jerónimo. The last to leave were the secretary and the steward.

They set off together, early in the morning, and together they went through the oak forest towards Puerto Nuevo, and slowly, without tiring their horses, they climbed to the pass. Behind them spread the Vera like a great green stain, tranquil and at peace.

At Tornavacas, after a few glasses of wine at the inn, the travelling companions separated. Don Gaztelu started on the road to Madrid, laden down with documents, letters and minutes belonging to Charles, that were to be handed over to the young monarch, while the other headed towards Valladolid.

So it was that Don Luis rode alone through towns and villages in mourning, for the news of the king's death had spread throughout Spain. But the further he got from Yuste, the more he felt oppressed by all that grief. The black-draped churches, the clangour of the bells which in one place after another kept time with the prayers of the people, affected him like echoes in an empty room.

Magdalèn also was dressed in mourning, and a black mantilla framed her pallid, perfect face. She embraced her husband with devout admiration, because he had been witness to a moment of such solemnity.

"You can't know yet how generously the court in Madrid has rewarded your loyalty to the king," she said, taking him by the arm and leading him to their room. "This separation has cost us all a lot, and I can scarcely imagine how you suffered, what with being so far away, and then your illness. We learnt about that afterwards, much later, when, thank God, you were out of danger. But anyway," and she gave a sigh of relief, "that time is over and done with, and you're back home for ever, my belovèd Luis!"

Quisada did not stop to ask what form Madrid's generosity had taken. He gazed at the miniature patio of the house and tried to expel the overpowering image of the walls of Yuste. Magdalèn's thoughtfulness freed him from the trouble of finding somewhere to put his few belongings. But while he was sitting on the edge of the bed, resting for a moment, she came across to him with the big package she had found among his clothes. She was staring at it uncomprehendingly.

"Those, Magdalèn, are some old documents that no longer have any value. In fact, it would be best to burn them. Is the kitchen fire alight?"

He got to his feet and took the emperor's manuscript which Don Gaztelu had hunted for in vain in every nook and cranny of the monastery.

In the fireplace there were more embers than flames, and over these there was a pot of water keeping warm. The hidalgo moved it aside and dropped the entire volume on to the glowing mass. In a trice the flames licked up, darting and sinuous, dancing before Quisada's eyes, then coiling down, then rising again, and finally, quietly, dying into the red of the embers.

Don Luis replaced the pot and left the kitchen. In the main room, shut up in semi-darkness to keep it from the sun of a summer afternoon, the big fireplace was empty and swept perfectly clean, except that on the gleaming firedogs were two logs which would not be burnt until late in the autumn. The hidalgo sat down before them, and put his feet up on the stone edge of the fireplace. He noticed that his boots were worn and dusty. He bent, and vainly tried to rub away all the dust with his hands.

When Magdalèn came downstairs she found him staring misty-eyed into the fireplace. She threw her arms round his shoulders.

"Ah, my Luis!" she said.

ORDER IN THE HOUSE

DURING THE NIGHT of August 14th–15th Herr Kölner was struck by paralysis. When the manservant entered the room in the morning, and realized the condition his master was in, Herr Kölner must have been lying like that for many hours. His gaping, terrified eyes were staring at the door: the only signs of life in a body distorted and immobilized. It did not even cross Anton's mind to approach the bed. Instead, he rushed down the stairs, breathlessly told the housekeeper to inform the mistress at once and, seizing hold of the telephone, tried to get in touch with the doctor.

The Kölner mansion was situated in a quiet district a few miles out of town. The horse-drawn trams passed right by the end of the drive, joining the bosky suburb to the heart of the city in less than half an hour. Herr Kölner travelled for the most part by this means, for he hated and feared the automobiles which were beginning to be seen around with increasing frequency. It must be said that his connections with the city had slackened off considerably: since he had built that house he had maintained only a few formal links with his former acquaintance in town. All the same, he continued to think it a duty to take himself off once a week to the Café Central.

There, on the very morning of August 15th, news of the appalling tragedy which had struck Kölner down spread like wildfire. The café tables were largely occupied by gentlemen waiting either for lunchtime or for High Mass in the cathedral; and Kölner should have been one of these. Ever since his children had drifted away from religion, and he himself had lost, or allowed to lapse, the habit of attending major church functions in the company of his wife, it had been his custom to come into town alone and dally for half an hour at the café. There he would browse casually through the newspapers and then stroll off at leisure towards the cathedral square. He always made a point of being in good time for church because he was distressed by flurry, and even more by the vexation of inadequately following the service, without a clear view of the altar or the priest. For this reason he would choose a front pew in the centre nave.

"We shan't be seeing him again," was the bland comment among the habitués of the café, mostly said as small-talk but with a dash of regret, for no one had ever been really close friends with him.

"He'll get over it," said others. "A man of his fibre doesn't give in easily. Even if he doesn't recover altogether, he'll adapt himself to things. Just you wait and see. One gets used to anything."

Meanwhile, in the room on the first floor of his suburban mansion Herr Kölner, in spite of having received first aid from the doctor, was still lying in the same appalling inertness.

The diagnosis, after a rapid analysis, was unequivocal: the malady had struck with ferocious force, leaving the upper and lower limbs completely paralysed, weakening the hearing and disabling the vocal cords. Indeed, from the mouth, twisted into a leer, there emerged no further sound.

[135]

"Is it possible that you can't do anything at all? Is there no cure?" Frau Kölner spoke with angry scorn and vexation: in the consternation of the moment she appeared to have forgotten the presence of the invalid who, in the same room and only a few steps away from her, could be described as cast out from the land of the living, lying in an incommunicable limbo of his own.

To put it bluntly, Helene Kölner was indignant. She, like the rest of the household, had never imagined it possible that a man still in his prime, a healthy man, could slip into such a terrifying abyss. And no one now thought of wondering what was going on in that man's mind.

The doctor advised removal to a clinic.

"What can they do for him in a clinic?" asked Frau Kölner.

"I don't think they can do much at all. In the present state of medicine our ability to help a patient as gravely ill as this is really minimal. But they could study the progress of the disease, examine it, and (who knows?) perhaps in time find a remedy."

"My husband shall not leave the house in this condition."

The woman's obstinate stance took the doctor by surprise, revealing an aspect of the situation which it had not occurred to him to consider. Herr Kölner's condition, rather than upsetting his wife, seemed to offend and embarrass her. The doctor took her politely by the arm and led her from the room, closing the door behind them, so that only faint echoes of an agitated conversation reached the patient; but he caught very little of it, locked as he was in pitiless solitude.

It was Saturday morning; the sky was heavy and whitish with oppressive heat. Herr Kölner should already have taken his place in the front rows of the central nave in St Stephen's. There were five minutes until the beginning of the celebration, the bishop had donned the sacred vestments and, along

[136]

with the four priests who would shortly form a garland round the altar, was immersed in prayer. At exactly eleven the little bell announced the beginning of Mass, and the subdued rustle made by the congregation rising to its feet to greet the celebrant echoed around in the dark vaults of the cathedral.

That same morning Frau Kölner summoned her two children, and with them agreed on the necessity of consulting the very best doctors – a consultation to be cloaked in the strictest secrecy. With her own hand she wrote letters to some of the most outstanding names in Austrian medicine: the high standing of her family was a recommendation sufficient to make the illustrious consultants hasten to obey her summons.

The doctor's first diagnosis was confirmed in every particular, and no one spoke of a cure, either immediate or in the foreseeable future. Karl Kölner was condemned to a life of immobility, and perhaps to silence, for ever.

Frau Kölner heard the sentence in the downstairs drawing-room, where the four doctors had been received and where, having concluded their examination, they were sipping cold tea. The appropriateness of the atmosphere and the impeccable professional correctness of these elderly gentlemen imposed a certain stiffness, which in the end was of assistance to them in the grave, delicate matter of informing a waiting wife of the unfortunately upsetting diagnosis after a long, detailed examination lasting more than two hours. When the bedroom door had finally opened, the footman waiting patiently in the corridor had ushered the four doctors into the drawing-room to serve them refreshments, announcing that Frau Kölner would be with them in a moment.

She entered a few minutes later and appeared to be calm, as austere as ever, and not in the least overawed by the situation. She hated to be dependent on others, and was even more irritated by the possibility that her moods and feelings were apparent to the eyes of strangers. She therefore habitually comported herself with rigorous restraint, adopting a cold detachment towards people and things, which in this particular moment of facing facts stood her in good stead.

The state of affairs was explained to her in detail, and to the best of her ability she followed the pronouncements of Professor Moser, but eventually she made an impatient gesture and interrupted that illustrious physician before he had summed matters up.

"Forgive my ignorance, doctor, but in plain words: how long can my husband expect to live in this state?"

The doctor gave a sigh before replying.

"As long as a person under normal conditions, madam. Your husband is not yet sixty and, however unlikely what I am telling you may appear, his physique is still unimpaired, and it will, in some manner, fight back against this blow."

"How can you say a thing like 'unimpaired physique' about that . . . that . . . And then, what keeps an individual alive, when it's in that sort of state?"

The word "individual" struck a sinister note with the four doctors, even though long experience of such maladies had often brought them into contact with tales of desperation and every sort of reaction and state of mind. For a moment they thought of the inert body of Karl Kölner, and visualized the lean, still-agile figure of the man, despite the change that had misshapen him. Above all, what was striking were the eyes. In those few days of immobility and silence they were already seeking some way of working out a rudimentary language. Or it may have been that the professional skill of the illustrious doctors had made them expert at penetrating and prying into such otherwise inscrutable silences . . .

"It could happen, madam, that the sense of hearing, which at this point has undergone only a slight deterioration, might be restored. The same is true of the vocal cords: with assistance and re-training they might be enabled to function again. On the other hand I cannot but understand your distress. It will be a labour of patience, vigilance and uncertainty. But your husband is an active, intelligent person, and will not remain totally inert for long."

Cold and evasive was the look she gave him, while she fiddled nervously with a solid gold bracelet engraved with an intricate Byzantine pattern.

It was the 18th of August, the very day on which Herr Kölner had arranged to set off for Italy. At 1745 hours, from the Südbahnhof, the train would be leaving for Villach, Venice and Milan. A fortnight earlier he had booked a sleeper as far as Verona. The train pulled out of the station right on time, and the empty place was occupied by a traveller who secretly thanked his lucky stars not to be having a rough ride of it, in spite of his lack of foresight.

In the suburban mansion, daily life resumed its course without any further disturbances, in apparent calm and rigorous good order. Helene Kölner had realized that order and order alone could ward off the disruption and awkwardness into which her husband's condition had thrust the entire family, and to this end she had devoted all her energies to building up a plausible sense of normality which would at least keep the uncertainty of the moment within tolerable limits. Of the future, of a more distant future, she did not wish to think.

She arranged that Anton, the servant who had first come to his master's aid, should be relieved of all his other duties and devote himself entirely to the invalid, whom he would not be permitted to leave except on his one day off a week. The good fellow made no objection at all to his change of role, but he was none the less concerned about taking on this truly disagreeable task. None of the servants had ever been in any way close to Herr Kölner: he was not the sort of person to ask for much help from his employees. The awe which Anton instinctively felt, as indeed they all did, was multiplied a hundred times by the new condition of his master, whose thoughts he was unable even to imagine, and to whom his presence, though essential, might well become displeasing, irksome and obtrusive. His attentions were going to be indispensable, but this meant nothing. Necessity generates no gratitude, and less now than ever.

As it turned out, Anton proved himself to be just the right person. From the start he performed his duties with great care, and as the days went by this care became less and less formal. The services he rendered his master, and the manner in which he carried them out, gave proof of exceptional patience; a discerning, sensitive kind of patience that no one would have imagined him to possess.

The days, presided over by the mistress of the house with a fixity of purpose, proceeded methodically. Towards the end of the morning came the doctor's visit, and for the patient that half-hour became the keystone of the day, or the link between him and the world, because only Dr Ober had attempted to find channels through which to make contact with him. He talked to him a lot, at great length, he talked about everything: and Herr Kölner perhaps showed signs of grasping certain phrases and tones of voice in that monologue. He fixed his gaze on the doctor's lips and read his words with all the determination of a semi-literate struggling to decipher a letter. The doctor could have sworn that some

[140]

of his eye-movements expressed a craving to reply; but it led to nothing. He ignored this and went on talking all the same.

In the afternoon, on the other hand, it was the lady of the house in person who kept watch over her husband. She sat by his side for hours, observing him and wondering what could possibly be the life-source of such inertia.

"Normal state of health!" she exclaimed to herself. "They don't know what they're talking about. He won't live much longer. This paralysis will do for him sooner than they think!"

Although she sat with him, she kept her distance from the bed, only occasionally putting out a hand to touch him or to straighten the sheet. Most of the time she spent reading, just to while away the hours. Every so often she would lower the book and eye her husband furtively, studying his distorted features. He seemed constantly in the grip of some heavy stupor, and he breathed slowly and laboriously through a twisted, half-open mouth.

At six o'clock (for the town clocks chimed away the hours of the afternoon for her) she rose from her chair and, whether he was asleep or not, and convinced of not being heard in any case, she murmured, "Well, Karl, it's time for me to see about the dinner." Then she put her open book face down on the bedside table, and left the room.

Herr Kölner had always detested that habit of hers: sooner or later the bindings fell to bits.

So passed the months of August and September. There were few visitors, and those few were rebuffed by the brusqueness of the family, reluctant to take their guests into the sickroom.

The Kölners belonged to the wealthy middle classes;

indeed they had pretensions of a foothold in the lesser nobility, and Frau Kölner in particular did not fail to nourish lofty
ambitions for her two children. Now, if the disability of the
head of the family in no way prejudiced the flourishing affluence of the household, none the less in some measure it
spoilt, indeed it poisoned, the prestige which the latter had
hitherto enjoyed. Inevitably she and the two young people
paid fewer visits to the salons in the city, and the house was
more quarantined than was strictly necessary. They rarely
received, and then only in private, as if the mansion were
"shadowed o'er by mourning", or at least by the imminence
of mourning.

But in the course of the next few months Karl Kölner did
not deteriorate in any way. His heart was holding up well, his
lungs, though sorely tried by his having to lie on his back the
whole time, continued to function energetically, while his
entire organism was slowly constructing an unforeseen
equilibrium of its own.

The autumn had dragged on, with mildish days and scat-
tered showers, so that the snow, though it did not begin until
early in December, caught everyone on the wrong foot. It
was sometimes heavy, it was sometimes light, but it did not
let up altogether until Christmas Eve.

It was during those days of expectancy that, in the depths
of the unfathomable silence of his affliction, Herr Kölner had
the impression of being able to make something out distinctly: there were sounds that reached him no longer con-
fused and muffled. With the sense and suspense of impossible hope, with patience, with stupefaction, he was convinced
of hearing echoes of household life less remote from him than
they had previously been: and indeed he really heard them.
More clearly he discerned the sound of the door swinging on
its hinges, while the footsteps approaching him were quite

distinct, as were the voices which, though speaking in undertones, reached him from the adjacent rooms. No longer mere scraps of words assembled from the movements of Helene's lips, or Anton's, but the familiar ring of their voices, the changes of timbre and inflection: these had returned to his ears.

This had not been a miracle that had happened overnight, but a slow progress in which he himself, prostrated by illness, had not really believed, but which now appeared to have been accomplished, or nearly so.

It was a family tradition that on Christmas night the Kölners, having wished the servants a happy, Christian holiday, would leave the house in a carriage and go into Vienna for Midnight Mass in the cathedral. After that they were guests in the apartment of Clara Bauer, Frau Kölner's elderly sister who had been living alone for ages in the family home. They lunched with her on Christmas Day and only returned in the evening. This custom was blessed a thousand times over by the servants, who had the whole day to themselves until late afternoon, when they prepared the evening meal, which was usually a frugal one, and busied themselves with getting the table ready for the big Boxing Day lunch.

Two days before the holiday, the morning post brought a short message from Fräulein Bauer to her sister:

My dear, I would come out myself to see you, and to wish every happiness to your husband as well, but the streets at the moment seem to me impossible, and taking a tram is really too much for me. Just seeing people pushing and shoving at the stop under my window is enough to put me off. But you will of course give Karl my greetings and good wishes, and so we will hope to spare him the pain of being unable to speak. I got the impression yesterday, from Hans and

Agnes, that you were in two minds about what to do on Christmas night. Needless to say, I am expecting you all after Mass in the cathedral. It doesn't seem to me right to let such a well-loved custom lapse; and in any case I can't see what good it would do Karl for you all to stay around him at home. Perhaps what he really needs is peace and quiet. All my love,

CLARA

So Christmas night Herr Kölner spent alone.

He had the servants nearby, as thoughtful as ever, only just a little put out by the presence of the master, which might put a damper on their freedom. The joy of people who for one day in the year have the complete run of a place which at other times imposes limitations, was a trifle tarnished; but the jobs they had to do were actually very few, and habit had made them almost automatic. Moreover, once the patient's door was shut there were no further restrictions.

That evening Helene and the two children had come to say goodbye to him, and he had taken a good, long look at them, and noticed how awkward and impatient they were in his presence: especially the children, because they had never been really close to him, even before he fell ill. Rarely, and then only when they were very young, had they seen their father in bed, and now it embarrassed them, as if it were some slightly vulgar *faux pas*. Agnes already had her fur coat on, and had to take it off again because the room was so hot and the visit dragged on so. Now, as she held it over her arm, she did not sit down or even lean against the back of the chair in which her mother had made herself comfortable. As happens at the bedside of an invalid, the three of them spoke mostly between themselves, addressing him only occasionally. Hans, moreover, appeared to be particularly fascinated by the window, while his thoughtless gestures and

unthinking words betrayed his desire to be out of there
quick, and into the garden where the carriage was waiting, or
into the downstairs drawing-room, where you could breathe
more healthy air. Karl followed the direction his son's eyes
were taking, and detected his barely restrained, poorly concealed uneasiness. Had he been able to speak he would have
asked him, and indeed ordered him, to leave the room.

Anyway, Helene had risen from her chair and bidden him
a peaceful night. After her, it was up to Hans and Agnes to do
their bit. Eventually they all left, and then it was silence
indeed: through the window Karl observed the reflected
light of the snow on the nearby trees. The servants were
sleeping, while in the adjoining room Anton also was in his
first, deep sleep of the night.

By that time Frau Kölner and the children must already
have reached the cathedral square, illuminated with the bril-
liance of daylight. The great door of the church was crammed
with the throng which traditionally came crowding to that solemn celebration, pausing on the threshold to exchange greetings and to wait, while within there was a more discreet pat-
tering of feet, and greetings were confined to polite nods of
the head. Once again Herr Kölner thought nostalgically of
the warm, mysterious luminosity of the cathedral, and even
had a distinct image in his mind of the faces of the three
Church Fathers depicted on Pilgram's famous pulpit emerging from the semi-darkness of the lofty nave.

To the invalid's room Anton had brought a branch of
spruce in a shiny copper vase, and when he put it down on
the wooden chest it seemed at least a meagre gesture of good
wishes, and one which his master seemed to have particularly
appreciated. Next to it had been placed a valuable walnut
lectern, a present from his wife, a stylish object typical of
Helene. She had thought that later on, when he had

recovered some of his faculties, someone could stand it beside his bed, and remain there to turn the pages one by one. Karl had looked at it and admired it, reflecting bitterly upon its useless elegance.

Effortlessly he allowed himself to slide into the quiet of night. The previous evening he had had trouble getting to sleep, and even when he did, his sleep was beset with sombre, harassing dreams and continual nervous spasms, so that now he relaxed gratefully into the perfect calm. He enjoyed the small noises that broke into the isolation of his illness, and felt that he was in an impenetrable fortress, safe.

When the few days of holiday were over, and the doctor came back to visit Herr Kölner, he noticed a change that at first he was unable to explain. It was not that the patient's condition had visibly altered in any obvious way, but rather that the doctor perceived in him a calm of mind unusual in such a nervous organism. He decided to say nothing to the family, at least until that intuition had become more concrete and precise. Anton confirmed the fact that his master spent less of his time sleeping, and devoted a considerable part of the day observing whatever of the outside world could be seen from his bed. Over and above this (something that not even the vigilant Anton could realise) he had acquired a clear-cut impression of the changes taking place about him. He knew that his son Hans had asked for and obtained a motor car, while no one had thought of informing him about something so obnoxious to him, but he decided to attribute this silence to a feeling of discretion towards his person. He also found discreet his wife's decision not to sit at his side every single afternoon, and he devoted himself the more easily to looking through the window and observing the thaw as it lightened the burden of the pine trees.

One morning, during Dr Ober's visit, the servant entered the room with a basin of hot water, which he inadvertently caught against the marble table-top. At the faint tap of the china Herr Kölner gave a visible start. The doctor vouchsafed him a long gaze of enquiry, but said nothing. He waited for Anton to leave the room, slowly completed his visit, then put his instruments away in his bag.

"I'll be round at the same time tomorrow." He was aware of having pronounced the phrase with more care than usual. "Perhaps the time has come for us to make a change in your circumstances. Am I right, Herr Kölner? I will mention as much to your wife." And although he spoke in his habitual tone of voice he himself perceived a new ring in what he said, that of someone who for the first time has pierced a wall of silence.

Dr Ober left the Kölner house with a grave weight on his shoulders. He had glimpsed the lady of the house in the room leading off the vestibule, but he had not spoken to her. For some strange reason, a superstitious caution perhaps, he did not feel ready to bring the subject up with her. In years of doctoring he could not remember ever having felt such an overwhelming need to escape from someone.

The gardener had shovelled the snow off the drive, and the passage up to the house now appeared as a broad grey strip, perfectly straight though widening out at the gate like an estuary. Dr Ober thought of the futility of such a labour, since the white sky was still heavy with snow and the present calm would not last until evening. Without waiting for the tram, he set off at a brisk pace towards the city.

The following day Helene Kölner did not stay in to await the doctor, and throughout the week an odd series of coincidences cropped up to frustrate the intentions of Dr Ober, who no longer had the remotest doubt about his patient's improvement. In the visits which had followed the one which Dr Ober still remembered with incredulous amazement, one thing after another had confirmed him in his opinion, though he still felt it his duty to keep this secret. He realized that he was even afraid lest some trifle might betray the patient's new condition in front of Anton.

Not until the beginning of the next week did Dr Ober meet the lady of the house: or rather, he ran into her as she was entering the hall, chilled and half-hidden in her hat and furs.

"This winter's never going to end," she complained with the hint of a smile, shaking off the evidence of the umpteenth snowfall. The doctor seemed embarrassed and edgy, so Frau Kölner asked him to sit down and have a cup of tea with her. She led the way into the drawing-room, and she gave a shudder at the heat of the stove in there.

"So then, what can you tell me about my husband's state of health?" she asked after a pause, warming her hands on her cup.

"That would be a complex matter to report on, madam, although for some time now I have been wishing to mention to you that . . . because, you see, on the clinical level . . ."

"Let us drop this kind of language, doctor, I beg of you. You know perfectly well that I am unable to follow you. In a word, is my husband getting better? Or is he worse?"

The bluntness of the question was nothing new to Dr Ober. Indeed, he had learnt to decipher the veiled message which it contained, the most secret and repressed of all Frau Kölner's desires. He surprised himself thinking that this woman, so icy and self-controlled, could not help arousing in him a disquieting feeling of pity: seated on the edge of his chair, apparently embarrassed and out of place, deep down he felt himself to be the secret tyrant of the *grande dame* opposite him, who was fondling the bun at the nape of her neck with slow, complacent gestures.

"You will remember, of course, that Dr Moser spoke of your husband's organism as a body which was, in a manner of speaking, healthy. At that time you could scarcely believe it, but now, five months later, you have proof of it. Herr Kölner's physique is responding perfectly, and has created a new way of living and reacting."

"But even if his body is, as you say, healthy – excuse me for interrupting you – my husband is none the less a finished man." Helene had become excitable as they spoke, and Ober observed to himself how the crudeness of the expression the woman had used gave the sense of having been prepared and meditated on for some time. He preferred not to dwell on this, but rather to follow up his own train of thought.

"That was just what I wished to speak to you about. I now think that it is no longer permissible to confine your husband's life to his bed. There are signs of great improvement. With sufficient help (and I'm certain that his spine will stand the strain) he could leave his room; and, when the weather improves, it would be a good thing to get him out into the garden. And later, why not even take him as far as Schönbrunn? Herr Kölner has always loved the garden, and going for walks."

"Ah yes, he enjoyed them very much. But, if I may be absolutely frank, to take him to Schönbrunn is in my opinion downright madness," the woman replied calmly. "Anyway, my dear doctor, the winter still stretches ahead of us. We'll talk about this later on . . ." And she looked outside at the heavy snowfall which had put the garden to sleep.

From his bed, Herr Kölner also looked out at the fresh snow on the topmost branches of the fir tree, and listened to the rhythmical scrape of the gardener's spade on the gravel driveway.

The weather chose to give ear to the secret prayers of Frau Kölner: even in mid-April the winter had not yet released its grip, and in fact was increasingly wild and biting. Since the condition of the invalid, his precarious "good health", as his lady wife sarcastically put it, did not allow of overbold experiments, that change which had been suggested and promised at the end of January was postponed indefinitely. The incessant rain which followed the snow had cleared the garden of the last patches of dirty white and the lawn was a vivid green, but the flowers were slow to appear. The magnolia had swiftly dropped its chalky-pink petals and was now arrayed in lucent, green leaves. It was Karl Kölner's favourite among all the trees they had planted years ago, when they first came to live there. The delicate handling it required, the efforts needed to shield it from the north wind and from sudden changes of temperature, had made its first few years of life precarious, and that it flowered at all was almost a miracle. Then the stem had grown sturdy, there was no more need to build shelters around it, and from season to season the young tree had greeted the delighted eyes of master and gardener with a lithe but ever more sturdy growth. Herr Kölner could not see it from his window, but he imagined it there, washed by the incessant rain, with the foot of the trunk beset by its own petals, smudged now and trodden underfoot.

But at last, with a sudden leap, the winter became late spring, and the moment for a change came even for Herr Kölner.

Late one sunny morning the wheelchair was brought into the sickroom and, under the eye of the doctor and of the mis-

tress of the house, the patient left his bed. It naturally fell to
Anton to lift the invalid and settle him in his new position.
The footman was a robust fellow, accustomed to heavy work
and adroit in his movements; all the more so because for
months he had been taking such care of his master. But it
required all his strength to lift the dead weight of that body,
enfeebled and emaciated as it was, and to place it carefully in
the chair.

Leaning against the chairback, trying to sustain the considerable effort of keeping his balance, Karl felt such a sharp,
piercing pain in his back that it brought tears to his eyes. It
lasted for a minute, or perhaps much less, he couldn't tell.
The others were unaware of it, while he himself, utterly
immobile, stared straight ahead at a black, burning spot.

Then he felt the gentle, capable hands of Dr Ober easing
his shoulders into position. He watched them gently laying
his forearms on his lap, on the edge of the rug tucked round
his knees. Helene, standing erect before him, looked on in
silence.

New, though minimal, changes took place in the series of
minute rituals which marked the hours of Herr Kölner's day.
In the morning they would take him to the room at the end of
the corridor, near the large east-facing window, where the
lukewarm sunshine spread in vivid stripes across the woollen
rug, and the inert, diaphanous hands of the invalid were
infused with a golden luminosity. Anton was on hand to min-
ister to him at breakfast, which was served by a maid who
retreated into a corner where she waited until she could
remove the tray. His wife arrived later on, to wish him a good
morning. She came quietly into the room, when Anton had
already gone back to the kitchen. She slipped through the
half-closed door, practically sneaked in, and sometimes took
time to dwell upon the appearance of her husband, whose

head she could see propped carefully against the tall back of the chair. Anton had placed this as near as possible to the open window, so that his master could see into the garden, and indeed he strained his eyes to see as far as he possibly could, all the way to the road at the end of the drive.

It happened one morning that Frau Kölner stood there behind her husband for longer than usual, and she saw him, slowly and with vast exertion, attempt to turn his head towards her. The prodigious effort of such a simple movement scared her so much that she hastened to prevent it, going right up to him and looking him in the eyes, though without being able to utter a word. Karl's eyes, on the other hand, looked to her so resolute, so imperative, that for the first time in months she was certain that he wanted to tell her something. A shudder went through her whole body, and mechanically she closed the window, mumbling about how stupid it was of Anton. When she turned to her husband again he had let his head fall back against the chair, and his eyes were closed.

He reopened them when he heard the slam of the hall door, and shortly afterwards he saw Helene on the drive. She was walking quickly, looking down and hurriedly buttoning up a glove.

One of Frau Kölner's special features was her elegance; and, since she was a shrewd woman, out of this quality so largely concerned with outward appearances she had created a lifestyle. The cut and colour of her clothes were not, when displayed on her, mere accessories, but rather the expression of a mentality formed in the very innermost citadel of affectation. On this understanding, at scarcely more than twenty, she had welcomed Herr Kölner as a husband. The reserved, uncommunicative distinction of a man much her senior had seemed to her attuned to the aesthetic cult on which she had modelled herself. It had taken a long time, alas, to reveal the basic misunderstanding which underlay the marriage of Karl and Helene Kölner, but time itself had shown that there was no need to undermine an order of things by then consecrated by the years. This was, in any case, a matter on which the two of them had never had occasion to dwell. Herr Kölner, in fact, had become decidedly reticent on the point. Whether from bitterness, or from convenience, was something Helene had never thought of asking herself.

On the tram which bore her towards the city centre she fixed her gaze dispassionately ahead of her, disregarding the people seated on either side of her, towards whom she felt not a morsel of curiosity. She was more inclined to meditate on Dr Ober's oft-reiterated suggestion that Karl should be taken to the Schönbrunn gardens. This would have been purely laughable had she not been rattled by the insistence of this doctor: he simply refused to understand how out of the question it was. Could it be *possible* that he had no idea of the sympathetic inquisitiveness of people, the brazen intrusiveness to which the patient would be subjected on account of his twisted figure, his distorted features? She would never consent to any such indecorous proceeding where her husband was concerned.

She got off the tram at the edge of the Ring, cut through the Hofburg gardens and reached the old town. There she went to a pastrycook's, attracted the attention of one of the aproned girls in starched white caps, and ordered a selection of biscuits. With these, a few minutes later, she presented herself at her sister's house.

It was some time now since Helene had taken to visiting Clara more frequently, in particular when it seemed that the atmosphere at home was growing too oppressive, and when an outing of an hour or two enabled her to put aside the thought, and indeed the sight, of her husband.

"Dr Ober," she told Clara when the two of them were sitting at table for a light lunch, "is insisting on the idea of taking *Karl* in a *carriage* to Schönbrunn. I don't have to say that I've told him countless times that it's just *too* absurd. I can't imagine how a doctor can be so utterly tactless! In any case, the children would never allow it for a moment, and speaking for myself I don't see the need for it."

She looked at her sister, expecting agreement. Clara would think the way she did, of course. But Clara did not reply immediately.

"One would need permission from the Imperial Chancellery, but that is easy enough, I can assure you," she said at length, concluding her thoughts out loud.

"What do you mean? What are you saying?"

"You know perfectly well that private carriages are not allowed in the gardens except by express permission of the royal family. On the other hand, I don't see how you could otherwise cross the whole courtyard all the way to the fountain, or reach one of the side-alleys . . . not with someone in Karl's condition. You need to take him in a carriage right up to the palace, and from there Anton could perfectly easily wheel him up and down the alleys in the invalid chair."

"But Clara, I don't understand you!"

"You don't? But it's perfectly simple. I agree with you, not to take him when the garden is crowded, but otherwise . . . It seems to me a good idea, Helene, and I think you're getting flustered about less than nothing. Would you like me to see to it?"

It was in great perturbation that Frau Kölner left her sister's house some hours later, and boarded the tram. Once more she felt that the calm she had struggled to force on herself, and had achieved after all those anxious months, was slipping from her grasp. In a moment of inattention she passed the tram-stop by her house, and only realized her mistake when the vehicle turned into the avenue which led straight up to the yawning gates of Schönbrunn. It struck her as a sign of malevolent destiny and upset her not a little, but there was nothing for it but to alight outside the palace gates and wait for a tram to take her back.

There was no one at the stop, and the tram coming up from the main road was not yet in sight. To pass the time she walked up the avenue towards the palace. The forecourt was deserted, and the yellow façade of the building screened her view of the gardens themselves. She wandered idly beneath the colonnade to the door of the palace, and came out on the side overlooking the gardens. At the end of the dead-straight line of cypresses, high on the hill, the black bulk of the Gloriette stood silhouetted. It was early afternoon: there was not a living soul in the park.

She watched the dark carriage approach the palace steps, saw Anton get out and, with the help of the coachman, extract the inert form of Herr Kölner and deposit it in the wheelchair. Thereupon Anton started pushing the grotesque vehicle down the very middle of the dusty white avenue. Helene had drawn to one side in horror, closed her sun-dazzled eyes and shielded her face with one hand. When she opened her eyes again, just a moment later, the avenue was empty. Holding up the hem of her dress to keep it out of the dust, she returned to the tram-stop outside the gates.

She reached home early in the afternoon, asked after no one, and shut herself in the study on the ground floor; and there she scribbled a few hasty lines to her sister. In spite of the urgency of the matter, she preferred the privacy of a letter to the speed of the telephone.

Then she sent for her son and ordered him to hurry to Fräulein Bauer's. She adopted a tone of voice which Hans could not remember having heard for some time, at least not addressed to him, and he obeyed without a murmur. Half an hour later Clara was reading the brief message in which her sister thanked her for her solicitude, but begged her to make no move with the Chancellery. She gave no reasons, which in any case she would have had no time to write.

Helene then turned her thoughts to the question of how to dissuade Dr Ober for ever from entertaining the notion which he had been cultivating for months, much to the detriment of Karl and of the whole family. But for that, until the following day, she had time on her side.

Next day Frau Kölner confronted the doctor, and only the self-control of the one and the hauteur of the other prevented a matter on which both were furiously hostile from degenerating into a brawl. The animosity of the discussion did, however, render both of them completely incautious. They did not realize, for example, that the study door had been left open, or stop to think that in the room where Herr Kölner spent most of his time the door had been barely pushed to, for reasons of prudence. From the floor above, the invalid heard the excited voices and knew that he was the object of a stormy confrontation. Helene's obstinate refusal to let her husband leave the house was met by Dr Ober's insistence that his patient was in need of a change. It was not only Schönbrunn that was now at stake, but the pure air of a village high in the hills, the tranquillity of a different, a secluded place, such as would give strength to the invalid's sorely tried physique and raise his spirits. He himself, Dr Ober, offered to accompany the patient.

From his room Herr Kölner followed no more of the conversation. Perhaps they had lowered their voices, or else his mind wandered after other daydreams. He recalled a place in Italian-speaking Switzerland where, as a boy, he had once spent a holiday with his mother and elder brother. Not far from the St Gotthard Pass, it was nothing more grand than a village with a post-house and a little cemetery with a low wall and a gate that came scarcely up to his shoulder, so that it seemed to him like a garden in full flower.

There he imagined himself celebrating his fifty-eighth birthday, drinking a toast in Italian muscatel from a glass which Anton would hold to his lips . . . and he passed his tongue over them as if already savouring its sweetness.

There was silence in the house. Dr Ober had not come to visit his patient as he usually did. On the other hand, a little later, his wife came up, crossing the threshold with resolute steps. She halted when she saw the head lolling to one side, and recognized the stupor that was as usual befuddling Karl's mind. She circled carefully round him and smoothed out the cushions which Anton had plumped up rather untidily. The window was open again, and a light breeze entered, slightly ruffling the grey hair on her husband's brow. Helene closed the windows, very quietly this time, looking over her shoulder to see if the noise had disturbed Karl's sleep.

His eyes were closed and his face completely calm, as though he had no awareness of the outside world. Helene silently tiptoed from the room.